FRED'S WORLD

LADYBIRDS

STICKS

BESTEST ANGUS FOX

SNAILS CAMOUFLAGE

BROTHER FLOSSIE BRAVE OUTDOORS WORMS BUGS

DORMITORY

MUD

FLINT DANGER

MARSHMALLOWS

HEDGE CHAOS

POCKETS BISCUITS

HARMONICA WOODLICE

YELL BILLIE

NOISE

OXFORD
UNIVERSITY PRESS

Great Clarendon Street, Oxford OX2 6DP

Oxford University Press is a department of the University of Oxford.
It furthers the University's objective of excellence in research, scholarship,
and education by publishing worldwide. Oxford is a registered trade mark
of Oxford University Press in the UK and in certain other countries

Text copyright © Elaine Wickson 2019
llustration copyright © Chris Judge 2019

The moral rights of the author have been asserted

Database right Oxford University Press (maker)

First published 2019

British Library Cataloguing in Publication Data

Data available

ISBN: 978-0-19-275906-1

1 3 5 7 9 10 8 6 4 2

Printed in India

Paper used in the production of this book is a natural,
recyclable product made from wood grown in sustainable forests.
The manufacturing process conforms to the environmental
regulations of the country of origin.

ACTION STAN

ELAINE WICKSON

PICTURES BY CHRIS JUDGE

OXFORD
UNIVERSITY PRESS

↳ SUNDAY AFTERNOON PLANS

'In the beginning there was a load of nuffink, which suddenly exploded into dust and biscuits. Then all the dinosaurs were born, followed by jelly and monkeys.'

My younger brother Fred still hasn't got the hang of the Big Bang. Or evolution. The definition of which is: *A GRADUAL PROCESS IN WHICH SOMETHING CHANGES INTO A USUALLY BETTER FORM OF ITSELF.* Apart from younger brothers—they're only put on this planet to disrupt our Sunday afternoon plans with no intention of evolving into normal human beings ever.

Let me know when someone invents

COOL-O-METER

SUPERCOOL
CHILLING OUT
NO SWEAT
IN THE SHADE
COLD FEET
THIN ICE
LUKEWARM
HOT AND BOTHERED
SWEATING BUCKETS
TOTAL MELTDOWN

time travel so I can go back to last Sunday afternoon at the cake shop, to stop Fred doing what he was just about to do before I gave my order to the Cake Shop Lady.

TIME TRAVEL ALERT!

Last Sunday Afternoon at the Cake Shop

Me: 'HI. CAN I HAVE ONE EXTREMELY CHOCOLATEY DOUBLE CHOCOLATE CHIP MUFFIN, AND A SLICE OF EXTRA LEMONY LEMON DRIZZLE, PLEASE?'

Cake Shop Lady: 'CERTAINLY. AND THE THREE CREAM DOUGHNUTS?'

Me: 'EH?'

Cake Shop Lady points to the front of the cake cabinet which Fred has squeezed his head into, and licked the cream off an entire plate of doughnuts.

Me (blushing): 'OH. HE'S NOT WITH ME.'

Cake Shop Lady points to a sign stating <u>All Licks Must Be Paid For</u>, which I'm pretty sure they only put up when Frederick Albert Fox walked in.

TIME TRAVEL END!

Not only did I have to buy all three cream-deprived do█████, I couldn't eat them because: lick.

I PAID FOR CAKES I DIDN'T EVEN EAT.

And I'm a cake fanatic, so that's heartbreak in a sentence right there.

I like a cake. I also like a cake chart. Never pie. Always cake. Here's the breakdown of how Fred has managed to ruin Sunday afternoon plans for me in the past five weeks:

COOL-O-METER

SUPERCOOL
CHILLING OUT
NO SWEAT
IN THE SHADE
COLD FEET
THIN ON ICE
LUKEWARM
HOT AND BOTHERED
SWEATING BUCKETS
TOTAL MELTDOWN

FIVE WAYS FRED HAS RUINED MY SUNDAY AFTERNOON PLANS

Making me relocate all the snails in the park so people won't 'haxidentally' step on them

Selling cakes to raise money for a Giant African Land Snail, except we didn't sell any because Mum only bakes cakes with vegetables in

Supervizing his playdate with Flossie McGregor, who made me play 'prisoners locked in dungeons', until I wished I was a prisoner locked in a dungeon just to get away from them

Suffering his harmonica practice while trying to write my 'Pluto IS a Planet' essay to send to the International Astronomical Union

Cake Shop Lick Debacle

CUT to *THIS* Sunday afternoon and there's a new one to add: *we're packing for the school trip.*

Well, I'm packing, while Freddie fills his suitcase with biscuits, toast (with jam on), and a tub of mint choc chip ice cream.

'Sure you don't need any jumpers, Fred?'

'Nope.'

'Or pyjamas or a toothbrush?'

'Flint Danger never needs a toothbrush.
He just packs bravery.'

Flint Danger has got a lot to answer
for. Fred's favourite programme is
DANGER QUEST, with the world's most
awe-inspiring adventurer:

'I'VE ROARED WITH LIONS, SWUNG
WITH MONKEYS, EATEN GROSS-LOOK-
ING BUGS, AND HAD SCORPIONS LIVING
ON MY FACE. I'VE SWAM SHARK-IN-
FESTED OCEANS WITH A BROKEN LEG,
AND DRANK MY OWN PEE EVEN WHEN
I DIDN'T HAVE TO. DANGER BY NAME,
DANGER BY NATURE.'

Flint Danger spends a lot of his time
eating and drinking things you wouldn't
find in the supermarket.

'TO SURVIVE IN THE WILD YOU
NEED TO LIVE ON THE EDGE,' he says,

COOL-O-METER

SUPERCOOL

CHILLING OUT

NO SWEAT

IN THE SHADE

COLD FEET

ON THIN ICE

LUKEWARM

HOT AND BOTHERED

SWEATING BUCKETS

TOTAL MELTDOWN

abseiling into a volcano with no shoes on
and barbecuing a tarantula. 'DANGER IS
IN MY DNA.'

To be honest, Flint Danger's DNA is
mainly suntan and denim. And it's all his
fault we're off to the woods for a few
days—Fred thinks Danger is in his DNA
too, and he's not far off:

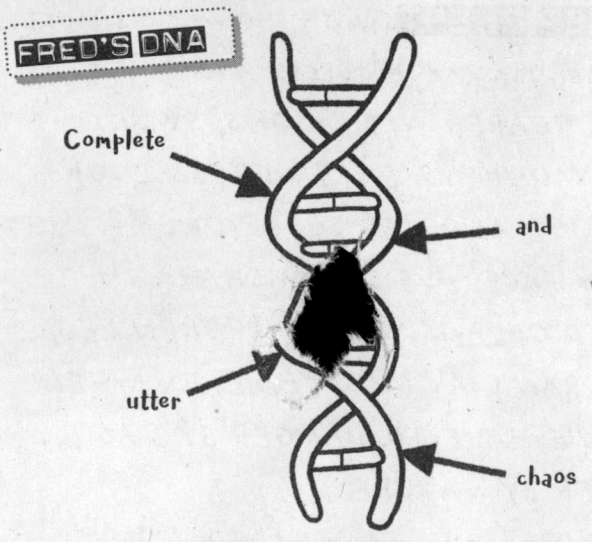

FRED'S DNA

Complete

and

utter

chaos

'We're going to live on the hedge in the
jungle all by ourselves,' Fred says, packing his
loo-roll binoculars. 'There'll be cock-a-doos,
meringue-a-tangs, and man-eating penguins.'

'We're going down the A420 to the local

wood, Fred, with about a billion parent helpers. And penguins are naturally found in Earth's southern hemisphere,' I say, remembering the episode where Flint Danger lived with a colony for a week to prove how manly he was.

It's a shame Fred isn't in Earth's southern hemisphere too.

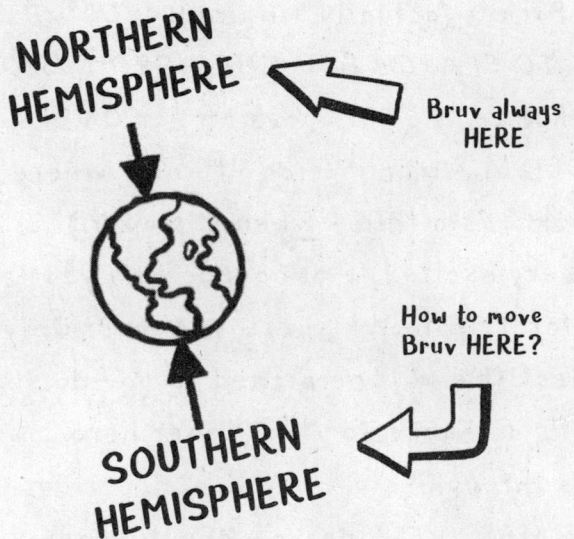

NORTHERN HEMISPHERE

Bruv always **HERE**

How to move Bruv **HERE?**

SOUTHERN HEMISPHERE

It's also a shame I didn't spot the danger of this trip. If only I could have gone back in time before Mrs Parker interrupted our water cycle lesson a few weeks ago, so

COOL-O-METER

SUPERCOOL

CHILLING OUT

NO SWEAT

IN THE SHADE

COLD FEET

ON THIN ICE

LUKEWARM

HOT AND BOTHERED

SWEATING BUCKETS

OWN

I could go to the loo and miss the whole thing:

TIME TRAVEL ALERT!

A Few Weeks Ago in Our Classroom

Mrs Parker (actually singing): 'YOU'VE GOT TO SEARCH FOR THE HERO INSIDE YOURSELF...' (This goes on for ONE WHOLE MINUTE. We don't know where to look. It's a relief when it's over.)
'I'm very excited to announce this year's Mentor Trip to Whispering Woods! Only a select few will be picked to go—do sign up; it's a chance for that inner hero to shine through!'

Cue MASSIVE slideshow about leadership and campfires. I almost nod off, until the slide about star-gazing grabs my attention.

Liam, who actually does nod off, suddenly wakes up and whispers: 'What's a Mentor

Trip to Whispering Woods?'

He may be my best mate, but he's forever oblivious. I wonder if he ever spends any of his life blivious.

Jess (rolling her eyes): 'They do it every year, you specimen. Some lucky Year Sixes get the chance to go away with the younger ones and help them learn about nature. It's about being all responsible and, y'know, not just how your hair looks.'

Jess is the only sane person I know, and spends half her life rolling her eyes at Liam.

Liam (restyling his hair): 'LUCKY Year Sixes? That sounds like pure tormenture, man-bro.'

Me: 'Um, a few days out of school with no Mr Fisher? Doesn't sound like pure tormenture to me.'

Our Year Six teacher Mr Fisher is a fun-free zone, and can detect a pencil doodling a pie chart, instead of writing about the ancient Greeks, from three miles away.

COOL-O-METER

SUPERCOOL

CHILLING OUT

NO SWEAT

IN THE SHADE

COLD FEET

ON THIN ICE

LUKEWARM

HOT AND BOTHERED

SWEATING BUCKETS

TOTAL MELTDOWN

Liam (now eating hula hoops): 'Count me in!'

Because Mr Fisher can also detect someone eating crisps from three miles away too, which is Liam's favourite pastime.

TIME TRAVEL END!

Little did we know it was going to involve writing a TWO-PAGE essay on why you should be picked, and raising the money to pay for your place. Liam did a sponsored wear-all-his-clothes-to-school-at-the-same-time, while I ran an after-school astronomy club. I was a bit miffed my oblivious best mate managed to raise all his money in one go, even though he had to be taken to the medical room for heat exhaustion.

And I wonder what on earth I was thinking, as I watch my little brother unstick half-licked lollipops off the wall and chuck them in with my socks.

But as Fred always says: 'YOU'VE ALWAYS WANTED TO EAT A MILKY WAY, HAVEN'T YOU STAN?'

Yes. Yes I have. Well, not *EAT* a Milky Way. *SEE* the Milky Way.

I'm crazy about space. I can't get enough of it (I can't get enough of the other type of space either, having to share a room with my brother). Stargazing in our back garden is useless. I'm pretty sure Mum's twenty strings of fairy lights can be seen from the International Space Station. And there's no chance of camping in a place remote enough to have a dark sky, because Mum won't go anywhere without 'A DECENT MÉS AND A PLUG SOCKET, STANLEY.'

A few nights beneath an unpolluted sky was too good to pass up.

'There will be tranchlas, won't there?' Fred asks, sitting on my spring-wear jumpers.

'I hope not.'

'What about lanky badgers?'

COOL-O-METER

SUPERCOOL

CHILLING OUT

NO SWEAT

IN THE SHADE

COLD FEET

ON THIN ICE

LUKEWARM

HOT AND BOTHERED

SWEATING BUCKETS

TOTAL MELTDOWN

'LANKY badgers?'

'Them black and white horsey fings.'

'You mean zebras?' I tut, lifting him out and replacing him with my comfiest pyjamas. 'Not down the A420.'

'What about knitted effalants?'

'Mammoths died out thousands of years ago, Fred.'

My brother's knowledge of wildlife is sketchy at best. His favourite book is TWO BY TWO, and he can't remember all the animals in that, despite it being only eight pages long and having been read to him every night since he's been alive. He thinks lav-lav snakes live in the toilet, robins are only alive at Christmas, and snails are appropriate pets to keep in the house.

'It's about time Angus had a holiday,' Fred says, having already packed lettuce.

Wherever Fred goes, Angus the snail goes, with a fetching felt-tip A splodged on the side of his shell so he can't get lost. He loves snails so much, they were the

top five things on his Christmas list. At least Angus is only three centimetres high, unlike Giant African Land Snails, which are bigger than your face and awake for most of the night. Thankfully Mum bought him a jigsaw instead.

She didn't say no to camp though, for obvious reasons.

'It'll be more fun than a bag of weasels!' she waltzes in, lifting Fred out of the suitcase and swapping the contents with stuff he actually needs.

'Fun for you maybe, with endless Mum O'Clock,' I sulk. 'You get to have time off Fred.'

'Today is another yesterday unless you grab life by the hands,' she says, quoting one of her bonkers fridge magnets. 'Besides, Fred will be no bother, will you pickle-pops?'

Mum holds his chin and tilts his face up to hers.

'As long as you use your indoor voice.'

COOL-O-METER

SUPERCOOL
CHILLING OUT
NO SWEAT
IN THE SHADE
COLD FEET
ON THIN ICE
LUKEWARM
HOT AND BOTHERED
SWEATING BUCKETS
TOTAL MELTDOWN

'But I'm gonna be outdoors,' he frowns.

'Exactly.'

Fred's outdoor voice is off the scale on the NOISE-O-METER.

ON THE SCALE

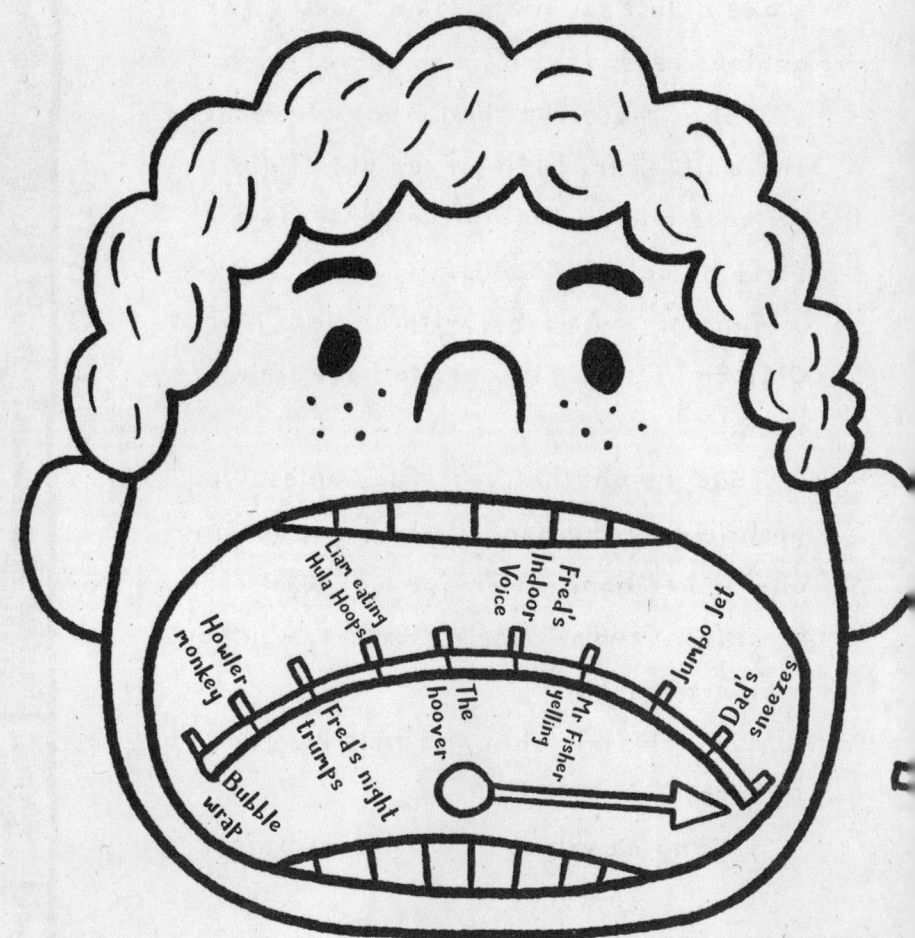

'You'll learn so much about yourselves, my little monkey-fleas,' Mum says.

I already know all I need to know about myself. I like plenty of me-time and preferably RIGHT NOW seeing as Fred has stripped down to his pants having packed everything he was wearing.

'Did you at least manage to get me a slouched beanie?'

According to Liam, it's an essential part of our campfire wardrobe, along with trainers that aren't canvas pumps handed down from one of my many cousins.

'I've got something better than a slouched beanie.' Dad walks in the room and hands us both a hat. 'The Knitting Ninja strikes again!'

OFF THE SCALE

Fred's Outdoor voice

COOL-O-METER

SUPERCOOL

CHILLING OUT

NO SWEAT

IN THE SHADE

COLD FEET

ON THIN ICE

LUKEWARM

HOT AND BOTHERED

SWEATING BUCKETS

TOTAL MELTDOWN

He's become so obsessed with knitting
lately, everything he gives us is made of
wool. So far I've been given a tank top,
a cape, arm warmers, and a snood. I don't
know what some of those things are. Surely
it's only a matter of time before I get
knitted pants.

Fred is excitedly wobbling his head,
showing off a bobble hat with an _F_ on the
front, and a bobble so humungous I wouldn't
be surprised if it caused a solar eclipse.

'You've got one too!' Dad pops it on.
Except mine has a letter _S_.

'Now everyone will know you're related
when you sit around the campfire!' He slaps
me on the back, as Fred jumps around the
room completely nude, having packed his
pants too.

'Great,' I say, shoving it in my rucksack
and hoping it'll never sit on my head again,
while Dad persuades Fred to put some
clothes on.

The doorbell goes. Gran has dropped by

to see us off.

'You didn't think I'd forget, did you?' she whispers, pulling out a package wrapped in string. 'Salted caramel brownies for the midnight feast.'

I can always rely on Gran for cake. Unlike Mum, who only ever puts vegetables in hers, including just lately parsnips. I'm <u>THIS</u> close to taking her to court for crimes against cake.

'I'll take care of those,' Mum says, grabbing them and fumbling with my rucksack.

'Don't forget, Stan . . .' Gran pulls me to one side. 'They'll tell you to stick to the paths, but if you do happen to wander off, always leave a trail behind you.'

She hands me a ball of red wool.

'They'll also tell you not to go in the woods at night, but if you do, use this.'

She takes out a head-torch.

'Keeps your hands free for hacking

COOL-O-METER

SUPERCOOL
CHILLING OUT
NO SWEAT
IN THE SHADE
COLD FEET
ON THIN ICE
LUKEWARM
HOT AND BOTHERED
SWEATING BUCKETS
TOTAL MELTDOWN

through the undergrowth and fighting off beasts.'

'We're only going down the A420, Gran.'

'That's what they all say, Stanley, that's what they all say.'

I gulp.

As soon as the car's loaded, we're on our way to meet the coach at school. It's too late to pull out now. That's what happens to your Sunday Afternoon Plans when you've got a little brother.

⤷ WOULD YOU RATHER?

The Milky Way is hidden from one third of humanity due to light pollution. It might also be down to Flossie McGregor's massive cloud of sugar-spun hair blocking out the sky.

Flossie is Jess's younger sister and Fred's best friend. Her hair often arrives five minutes before she does. She used to be the neighbourhood's only pirate captain, but now she's evolved into something else.

'Hmm . . . She inspects me with her magnifying glass as I walk through the school gates. 'I deduce spaghetti for lunch.'

'Flossie, I'm in a bit of a rush,' I say, noticing leftovers of Bolognese on my sleeve.

'I'm not Flossie! I'm Defective McGregor,

COOL-O-METER

SUPERCOOL

CHILLING OUT

NO SWEAT

IN THE SHADE

COLD FEET

ON THIN ICE

LUKEWARM

HOT AND BOTHERED

SWEATING BUCKETS

TOTAL MELTDOWN

NYPD!' She stamps her foot. 'And I'll crack this case if it's the last fing I do.'

'Whatever it is, it's nothing to do with me.'

She's already tried to crack two this month including Who Chucked Popcorn on the X13 Bus, and What's in Mrs Gravy's Gravy (case unsolved).

'You're the main suspect, wise guy.' She takes out a pad and pen from her unicorn rucksack. 'Where were you in the early hours of last week, when a great big scoundrel put a unicycle in our skip?'

'Not that it's any of your business, but I've never been near a unicycle.'

She narrows her eyes at me.

'It will be my business when forensics get back to me.' She curls her lip. 'I'll have you locked in the slammer and no mistake.'

I spot Liam and make a quick exit.

LIAM IS MY BEST MATE FOR THREE REASONS:

1. He's taller than me, which means he's great to hide behind when Flossie's waiting for forensics to get back to her.
2. He's never without Hula Hoops.
3. Splans. Special Plans. The secret of maintaining a good friendship is hanging out together and doing stuff like How Many Hula Hoops Can You Eat With Your Toes?

'Really hope you've got splans, man-bro,' he says, eating his way through a multipack. 'I'm not great at sitting on a coach for yonk-a-doodle-ages.'

'Luckily for you I have <u>PLENTY</u>.' I open my notebook. 'Including New Crisp Flavour Mash-Ups. I've already got a head start.'

COOL-O-METER

SUPERCOOL
CHILLING OUT
NO SWEAT
IN THE SHADE
COLD FEET
ON THIN ICE
LUKEWARM
HOT AND BOTHERED
SWEATING BUCKETS
TOTAL MELTDOWN

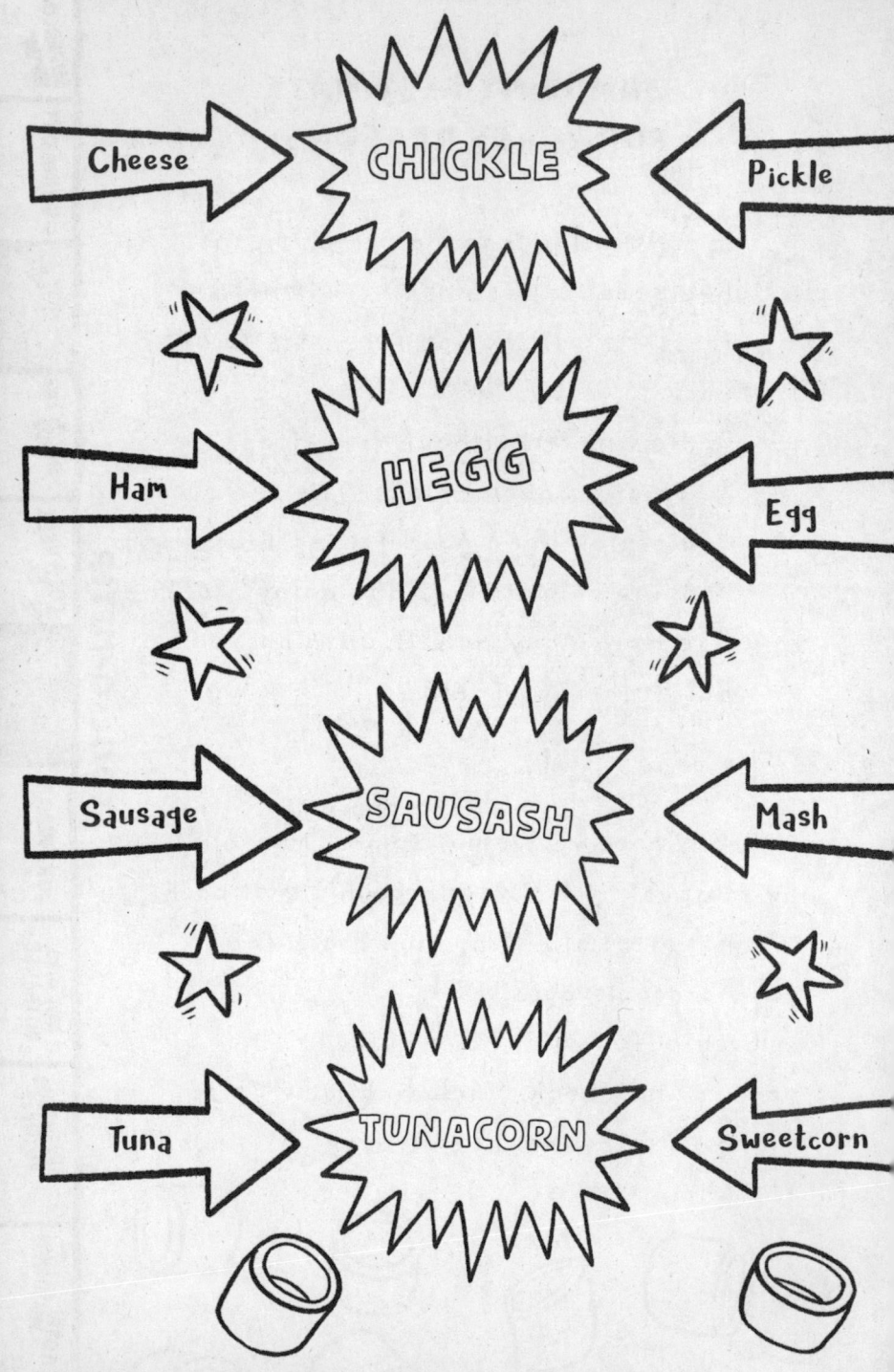

'That's inspired, Stanlington.'

'And I've got a fun word search of all the constellations we might see.'

'_FUN_ word search?' Idris tuts, taking out his phone. 'Those words don't go together. At least get some entertainment from the twenty-first century.'

Idris brings the tech to our friendship, whether I want it or not. He not only helps out the school's IT department (two computers and a broken mouse), he _is_ the school's IT department.

'I've already started filming the David Attenborough-style documentary that's gonna win me a BAFTA.' He zooms in on the pavement where there's a bit of squashed worm. 'Here in the remote jungles of Borneo we have the remnants of an eagle's dinner...'

Jess lifts her head from a book about the World's Most Amazing Zip Wires.

'Already I'm regretting being part of this trip.'

So am I, as we have to help load the

COOL-O-METER

SUPERCOOL
CHILLING OUT
NO SWEAT
IN THE SHADE
COLD FEET
ON THIN ICE
LUKEWARM
HOT AND BOTHERED
SWEATING BUCKETS
TOTAL MELTDOWN

bags of twenty small-year-olds, including Flossie's GINORMOUS unicorn suitcase which weighs like it might actually have a unicorn inside it.

'I'm wotching you mister,' she snarls at me. 'One wrong move and you're toast.'

'What EXACTLY have I done wrong?' I whisper to Jess.

'She's determined to crack the case of the Unicycle in the Skip.' Jess shrugs. 'And she saw you throw a load of rubbish into it on the way home from school.'

'I was putting stuff back in that had blown out!'

'Likely story.' Flossie magnifies her eye. 'Fings are starting to add up like a calculator.'

I quickly head over to Mum who's wiping Fred's face clean with a mum-spit tissue. She goes to do mine until I remind her of the contract I made her sign two years ago.

'Make sure you look after yourself.' She covers my face in kisses, ignoring

the clause I added to that
contract only yesterday
because I knew this would
happen. 'And look after Fred.
Don't let him climb trees, or eat dirt, or
lick toadstools, or bury vegetables, or, God
forbid, drink his own pee.'

'Have fun though, eh?' Dad rolls his eyes.

'I can email updates if you like, Mrs
Fox?' Idris offers, pointing to his phone.
'Take some footage of Freddie NOT
licking toadstools to put your mind at
rest.'

'Oh, that would be great, Idris. Um, are
you allowed to take that?'

'Between you and me, Mrs Fox, no.' He
taps his nose. 'But take this away from me,
you take away my lungs, know what I'm
saying?'

'Let's get on the coach.' I drag Idris
away, as Mum tells Fred not to eat all his
snacks at once.

I expected Fred to get a little teary as

COOL-O-METER

SUPERCOOL

CHILLING OUT

NO SWEAT

IN THE SHADE

COLD FEET

ON THIN ICE

LUKEWARM

HOT AND BOTHERED

SWEATING BUCKETS

TOTAL MELTDOWN

the coach departs, but he's too busy eating all his snacks at once. I'm about to settle back with my space-themed crossword, when Mrs Parker starts talking on the microphone.

'One-two, one-two... ahem. I have a little announcement to make.'

'This better not be another song.' Idris has his headphones at the ready.

'I'm sure we're going to have a WONDERFUL time in the woods,' she continues. 'Especially as another school will be joining us. Another school who will in fact be running the camp this year. What a great opportunity to make lots of new friends!'

'Which school, Miss?' Jess puts her hand up.

'Ahem-garkheel-ahem,' she coughs over a word.

'Didn't quite catch that.'

'Larkfield. It's Larkfield Primary.'

Even the parent helpers groan.

'I know what you're thinking.' Mrs Parker

stands up, and starts to play rousing music beneath her speech. 'Larkfield Primary, brilliant at everything, with their shiny imagination-stations instead of classrooms, and their shiny, youthful teachers fresh out of college. But . . . it's our time, Camford!'

She walks down the aisle as far as the mic will reach and shouts:

'For we can shine too! Bring it on!'

'You can't outshine the sun!' Liam shouts. 'Right Stan?'

'Um, I think there's a laser beam that can shine a billion times—'

'Well I never signed up for this,' Jess interrupts. 'And I like how she tells us now so we can't get off the coach. Larkfield are the best at everything AND they know it. I mean, they have a school cat called Einstein. We have carpet mites.'

'They don't have Mrs Gravy though,' Idris says, as though it's a good thing getting gravy with your school dinner, even when it's sponge pudding and custard.

COOL-O-METER

SUPERCOOL
CHILLING OUT
NO SWEAT
IN THE SHADE
COLD FEET
ON THIN ICE
LUKEWARM
HOT AND BOTHERED
SWEATING BUCKETS
TOTAL MELTDOWN

'At least Fisher won't be there—could be worse, guy-bros.' Liam shrugs.

It couldn't. We have such a big History with that school, it comes with a capital letter. And we come out the losers Every. Single. Time.

THINGS LARKFIELD HAVE WON

Maypole Dance-Off
☆
Clash of the Pronouns
☆
Egg & Spoon Showdown
☆
Algebra Play-offs
☆
Outstanding Onomatopoeia

Being the Best at Losing
☆

THINGS CAMFORD HAVE WON

'So, would you rather go on a school trip with Larkfield or poke sticks in your eyes?' Idris sighs. As well as being a techno whiz-kid, asking Would You Rather all day long is his other favourite pastime. I spend the rest of the journey answering sixteen of them, including: 'Would you rather have endless pancakes or magical hair?'

'Magical hair?'

'Your hair would always be cool, even on a windy day.' He looks at my hair. 'And even on a not windy day.'

'Definitely that then,' I say, trying to flatten the straw on my head.

Dad always says: 'YOUR HAIR IS MUCH LIKE A THATCHED ROOF, SON. IT'S A GOOD INSULATOR AND THE RAIN RUNS OFF IT, BUT IT STICKS OUT AT ALL ANGLES IF YOU DON'T GET THE PRO-FESSIONALS IN.'

'YOU COULD GROW IT INTO A MAN-BUN,' Mum once suggested.

'I COULD GROW IT INTO A SHEAF OF

SUPERCOOL

CHILLING OUT

NO SWEAT

IN THE SHADE

COLD FEET

ON THIN ICE

LUKEWARM

HOT AND BOTHERED

SWEATING BUCKETS

TOTAL MELTDOWN

COOL-O-METER

WHEAT,' I corrected her.

NOT ME

One thing's for sure: it would have looked a whole lot better with a SLOUCHED BEANIE.

I'm grateful when the coach pulls up and I don't have to choose between ketchup tears or nose custard, as we all shuffle off into the late afternoon sun.

'Hmm . . . it's very tree-y,' Idris says, filming the car park surrounded by woods.

There's no sound of traffic, just birdsong, and the crunch of feet on gravel as Mrs Parker and loads of parent helpers skip off into the trees with Fred and Co.

'OH NO!' yells Liam through a mouthful of crisps. 'WHAT'S HE DOING HERE?'

I spin around to see Mr Fisher marching over to greet us, carrying a rucksack so gigantic it's probably got its own moon system. He's dressed head to toe in beige. Well, I say toe, his shorts stop alarmingly at his knees—something I can't unsee.

'Liam Miller! Just because you're not in school, doesn't mean you can flout the school rules—stop eating!'

'What a nightmare . . .' Liam stuffs his Hula Hoops in his pocket.

'Miss Jefferson fell ill at the last moment, so I'm on the school trip instead,' he says, handing us a leaflet. 'I've put together some rules—this isn't a holiday!'

'No midnight feasts,' I read aloud. 'No talking after lights out, no messing about, no—'

'—way we're going to have fun,' Liam interrupts me. 'It's a nightmare that's actually happening in the daytime . . .'

COOL-O-METER

SUPERCOOL

CHILLING OUT

NO SWEAT

IN THE SHADE

COLD FEET

ON THIN ICE

LUKEWARM

HOT AND BOTHERED

SWEATING BUCKETS

TOTAL MELTDOWN

'Pay special attention to rule number twenty-five.' Mr Fisher points. 'NO WANDERING OFF CAMP or I will personally drive you home and have words with your parents and there'll be detention until the end of term. To help me keep an eye on you, you'll be wearing these.'

He pulls out a bunch of hi-vis vests from his rucksack.

'Oh my God.' Liam holds it up. 'It's got MENTOR written on the back of it. Sir, this seriously cramps my fashion style. There's no way I can wear—'

'Don't push your luck, Mr Miller, or I shall confiscate EVERY LAST CRISP you've got in your suitcase!' Mr Fisher's face turns a shade of sizzling pink.

Liam shrugs the vest on. If there's one thing we've learnt it's not to push our luck and move Mr Fisher up his **ANGRY SCALE**.

'It's a daymare. I'm having an actual daymare,' Liam complains, as we drag our suitcases through the wood until we emerge into a clearing surrounded by log cabins. 'Woah! Hammocks!'

He quickly forgets about his daymare and tries to climb into one with his gangly limbs.

And it's not just hammocks. There's a ring of toadstool seats around a campfire now occupied by Fred and his class. Signs point to 'fun this way' and 'happy vibes over here'. Wind chimes jangle in the breeze, and masses of fairy lights are strung from trees.

'Brilliant,' I say, gesturing to the light pollution.

'I can't see ANY sign of a zip wire,' Jess folds her arms.

Suddenly a bloke who's mainly beard skips into camp with a ukulele. He tries to jump over a toadstool but can't quite make it because of his tight skinny jeans.
Close behind him is a woman with

clouds of black curly hair, wearing baggy
jeans and rainbow braces, handing out
'welcome falafels'.

'Who are *THEY*?' Jess whispers.

'I think they're hipsters,' Idris says.
'Apparently they get through A LOT of
chickpeas.'

'Hey kids! We're Petra and Rufus! We
don't believe in labels. Everyone should
be free to be the best they can be, yeah?'
Rufus doffs his flat cap to Mrs Parker.
'That's our motto at Larkfield.'

'They're TEACHERS . . .' Liam's mouth
drops open. 'But, like, COOL ones!'

'Ahem.' Mr Fisher steps forward and tries
to hand over a ring-binder. 'I took the liberty
of photocopying some activity sheets.'

'Someone didn't get the chill-out memo!'
Rufus laughs, handing him a falafel instead.
'We do things differently at Larkfield. You
need to leave room for your students to
breathe—how else will they grow? Here, let me
explain, Norman. I'm sensing a uke situation.'

COOL-O-METER

SUPERCOOL

CHILLING OUT

NO SWEAT

IN THE SHADE

COLD FEET

THIN ON ICE

LUKEWARM

HOT AND BOTHERED

SWEATING BUCKETS

TOTAL MELTDOWN

'I prefer "Mr Fisher" in business hours.'

Rufus has already started playing the ukulele, as some Larkfield small-year-olds appear from the woods, breaking into a dance routine led by Petra, while Rufus sings about vibes and nature and artisan bread.

'THINK OF THIS AS SCHOOL IN A WOOD, WHERE THE TREES ARE YOUR WHITEBOARD, THE LEAVES ARE YOUR BOOKS—'

'Um, books will actually be your books,' Mr Fisher interjects. 'We don't want anyone writing on the leaves—'

'THROW AWAY RULES AND CHUCK AWAY PENS. TUNE INTO NATURE, MAKE ANIMAL DENS—'

Mr Fisher turns Cherry Blush at the prospect of throwing away rules, or maybe because Mrs Parker has started to dance along with several parent helpers. I wonder if it's too late to get back on the coach, and so does Jess, as we start edging backwards.

'At Whispering Woods we say

WELCOME BACK.' Petra beckons us to join in. 'For you already belong, yeah?'

'EXCUSE ME!'

A flock of birds takes off in the distance, Larkfield stop dancing, and everything goes quiet. It's Fred using his outdoor voice.

'DO I HAVE TO COMPLETELY WHISPER ALL THE WHOLE TIME?'

'Why little puffling!' Petra gasps, pushing her bright red glasses up her nose. 'You've startled the chiffchaff and the brambling. Harmonize those vocal chords or there'll be nothing left for you to discover.'

'LIKE BEARS AND VOLCANOES?' He karate chops the air. 'Cos I'm ready for them.'

'The only bear you'll see here is in the stars,' Rufus says, pointing at the sky. 'Whoever wins the GREAT BIG SCHOOL CHALLENGE gets to spend a night sleeping under Earth's ceiling.'

My eyes widen, but soon narrow again, as do Jess's.

COOL-O-METER

SUPERCOOL
CHILLING OUT
NO SWEAT
IN THE SHADE
COLD FEET
ON THIN ICE
LUKEWARM
HOT AND BOTHERED
SWEATING BUCKETS
TOTAL MELTDOWN

'Might have known there'd be a competition —it's all winny-win-win with them.'

'Let me break this down.' Rufus rolls up his sleeves, revealing armfuls of tattoos. 'This trip is all about INDIVIDUAL EVOLUTION. Everything you learn will be put into practice on the last day, so get in touch with your inner nature.'

'Um, I'm not sure I QUITE understand the rules.' Mr Fisher holds up his hand.

'SQUAWK!' Petra shrieks, flapping her arms. 'Here at Whispering Woods we like to discover our inner animals! I am a parrot—colourful, impressive, and massively energetic. SQUAWK!'

'And I'm a dolphin.' Rufus starts clicking and squeaking. 'Intelligent, gentle by nature, and I love a bit of mackerel on sourdough. What animal are you, Norman?'

He looks like a rabbit to me. Caught in the headlights.

'Trust me Norm; find your inner animal, and you'll three-hundred-per-cent this trip.

It'll be like your brain has been on holiday and come back with souvenirs. Same with you, mentors.' Rufus winks at us, and all we can do is side-eye each other, as Fisher tries to hand over some hi-vis vests.

'Oh, our mentors won't be needing those!' Rufus laughs. 'No labels, remember? You'll see they have their own style when you meet them.'

Petra leads us to the log cabins. I notice they have Larkfield-type names like Slumber Shack and Downtime Hut. Mr Fisher seems happier when he spots a porta-cabin with a flip chart in it.

'We call that the PORTAL Cabin,' Petra says. 'Put the right teacher in there, and you'll open up a world of pure imagination.'

'Pure boredomation if Fisher's got anything to do with it,' Liam grumbles.

We have until eighteen hundred hours to unpack and meet by the toadstools. Thanks to Flint Danger's endless quests, I know

COOL-O-METER

SUPERCOOL
CHILLING OUT
NO SWEAT
IN THE SHADE
COLD FEET
ON THIN ICE
LUKEWARM
HOT AND BOTHERED
SWEATING BUCKETS
TOTAL MELTDOWN

what that is: the twenty-four-hour clock
is an adventurer's best friend. It doesn't
leave much time seeing as I have to help
Fred unpack. The small-year-olds are in
a Slumber Shack with animal posters and
rainbow lights, and loads of parent helpers
just up the corridor.

'Well, this is nice and cosy,' I say.

'Flint Danger sleeps inside dead mooses.'
Fred flings the duvet on the floor. 'I want
a dead moose.'

'I'm sure this will be much comfier and
not so . . . moosey.'

Unfortunately I then witness him unpack.

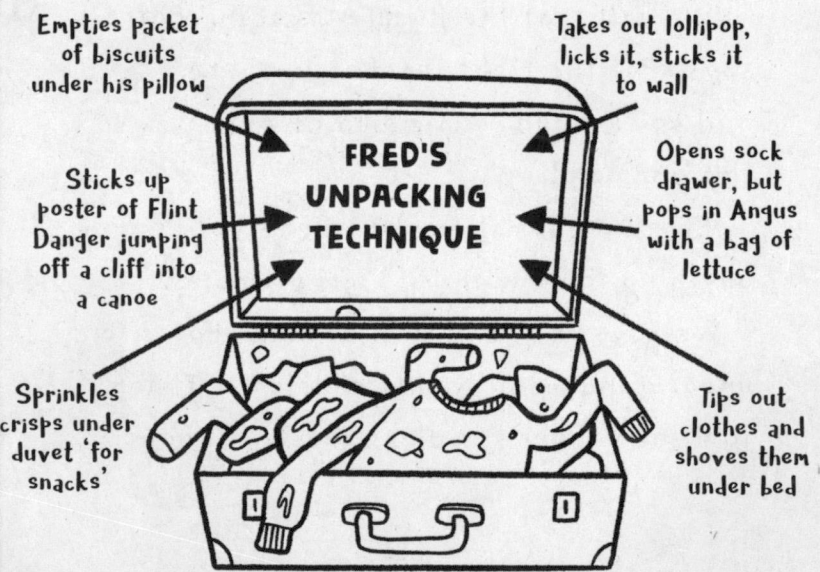

Empties packet
of biscuits
under his pillow

Takes out lollipop,
licks it, sticks it
to wall

**FRED'S
UNPACKING
TECHNIQUE**

Sticks up
poster of Flint
Danger jumping
off a cliff into
a canoe

Opens sock
drawer, but
pops in Angus
with a bag of
lettuce

Sprinkles
crisps under
duvet 'for
snacks'

Tips out
clothes and
shoves them
under bed

I'm thankful Year Six are sleeping in the other Slumber Shack. As I make my way out, I notice a constellation chart on the wall. I breathe in the log cabin air, which is a bit damp sock, but already I feel better about the prospect of stargazing and—

'Um, Stan, you appear to be leaking.'

My thoughts are interrupted by Mrs Parker, who's pointing to a trail of gloop behind me. It seems to be coming from my suitcase.

I quickly unzip it and fling it open.

'Oh. My. God,' I say, staring at the mess: my neatly folded jumpers are covered in sticky gloop; my socks are soaked; and my comfiest pyjamas are full of mint choc chips.

'Woah!' Liam shouts, from behind me. 'You've had a suitcase disastrophe!'

RECIPE FOR DISASTER
* 1 Fred
* 1 Suitcase
Stir in things that should be kept in the freezer

COOL-O-METER

SUPERCOOL

CHILLING OUT

NO SWEAT

IN THE SHADE

COLD FEET

ON THIN ICE

LUKEWARM

HOT AND BOTHERED

SWEATING BUCKETS

TOTAL MELTDOWN

He's right. Fred packed the ice cream after all. IN MY CASE.

⤷ WONDERS OF THE WORLD

Houston, we have a problem. OK, maybe not as big a problem as a major technical fault in Apollo 13's service module, but I've got ice cream in my pants.

At least I get to share a room with Liam and Idris, even if the bunk beds are a bit rickety and our room's next to the smelly toilets.

'Shame it melted. Could have added to our stash.' Liam flings open the wardrobe, which is stuffed with crisps and chocolate, and I add Gran's brownies from my rucksack. That's when I realize the only non-ice-cream clothing I've got is Dad's knitted hat.

Thankfully Liam's brought enough skinny jeans to last a month. Except he's taller than me so I end up with the world record of

COOL-O-METER

SUPERCOOL

CHILLING OUT

NO SWEAT

IN THE SHADE

COLD FEET

ON THIN ICE

LUKEWARM

HOT AND BOTHERED

SWEATING BUCKETS

TOTAL MELTDOWN

turn-ups, and a T-shirt down to my knees.

'How come my cool clothes hang different on you?' he frowns.

Because I've never been cool, as noted on my hastily drawn up **HAMMER STRIKE** (hastily drawn up because I realized that wasn't a cool thing to be doing either).

Roll up, roll up, come and see Stanley Fox _NEVER_ hit the cool bell.

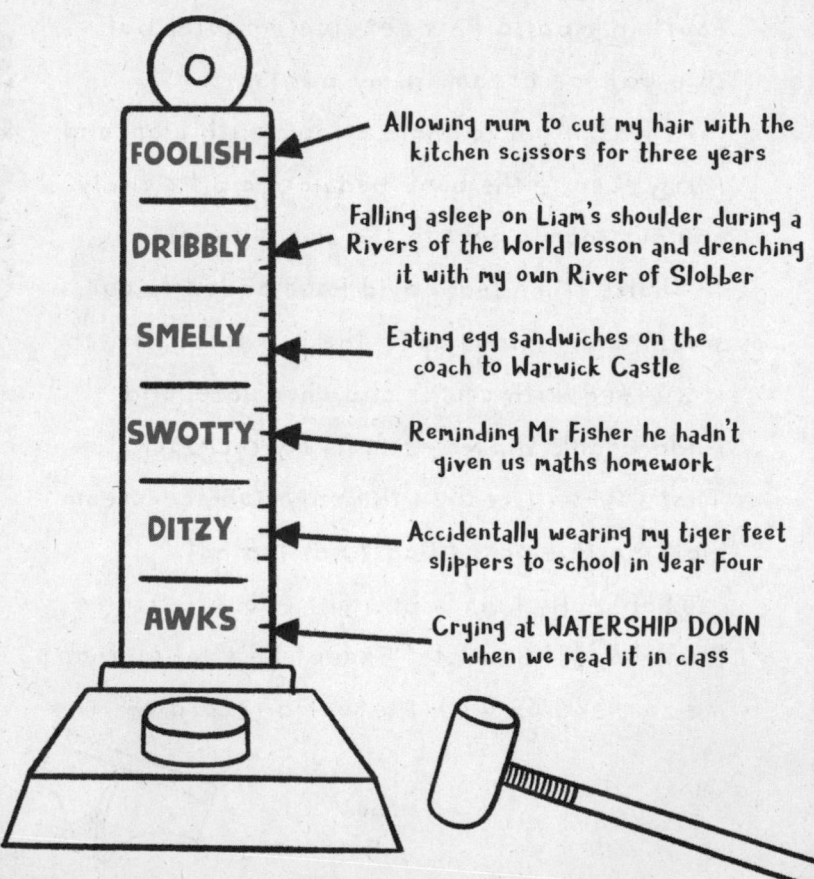

FOOLISH — Allowing mum to cut my hair with the kitchen scissors for three years

DRIBBLY — Falling asleep on Liam's shoulder during a Rivers of the World lesson and drenching it with my own River of Slobber

SMELLY — Eating egg sandwiches on the coach to Warwick Castle

SWOTTY — Reminding Mr Fisher he hadn't given us maths homework

DITZY — Accidentally wearing my tiger feet slippers to school in Year Four

AWKS — Crying at WATERSHIP DOWN when we read it in class

And now there's Leaky—trying to explain
to a parent helper why I needed to wash
ALL MY CLOTHES ON THE FIRST DAY, for
which I take all the blame so Fred doesn't
get into trouble.

I hang my clothes on the radiator and rush
off to the toadstools. Everyone's circling a
crackling fire, feasting on hot dogs. Except
Mr Fisher, who decided to pitch a tent and
is still trying to put it together.

'I'd rather be at one with the elements.
Nothing like the gentle baa of the lamb,
and the beautiful dawn chorus. Ah! The
countryside.'

Though it might be because he's trying to
get away from Rufus and his artisan teabags.

Fred has been playing THE TWELVE
DAYS OF CHRISTMAS on his
harmonica for the past five minutes. I
distract him with marshmallows, seeing
as his version goes all the way up to
TWENTY-SIX TRUMPETS TRUMPING.

Liam's got the right idea, hiding in a

COOL-O-METER

SUPERCOOL

CHILLING OUT

NO SWEAT

IN THE SHADE

COLD FEET

ON THIN ICE

LUKEWARM

HOT AND BOTHERED

SWEATING BUCKETS

TOTAL MELTDOWN

hammock and working on crisp mash-ups, although so far he's only come up with Snickeroni (Snickers and Pepperoni).

'I mean OK, they've got a book exchange,' Jess sighs. 'And there's an actual reading tree you can sit in, and a board games gazebo with Scrabble. But I want zip wires as well as a varied selection of paperbacks.'

'How do you even know all this?'

'Have you not studied the welcome pack?' she hands me a map of the camp.

'I was too busy getting ice cream out of my socks.' I shiver at the thought of my bare ankles.

'If you're cold, put your hat on.' She grabs it out of my pocket and puts it on my head. 'Oh!'

'I realize it's pretty embarrassing, with a bobble that could affect the tides of the sea, however a bit more support—'

'Not your hat—the Larkfield mentors. They're here,' she points.

I'm not sure if it's my imagination, but

the breeze seems to drop. All that can be heard is the crackle of fire, as we stare at each other across the camp. There's no hint of a wind chime, as they casually lean against trees in their sunglasses, though the sun set half an hour ago.

'WOAH!' Liam shouts, shattering the silence, and falling out of the hammock. 'He's wearing a SWIFTDRY Aviator jacket!'

'He's what?'

A boy walks towards us, the crowd parting as he does. He flicks his blond quiff, pulls up the collar on his leather jacket, and I'm pretty sure he'd stand in front of a wind machine if there was one available.

'You'd never catch me in anything not designer.' He lowers his shades and stares at my hat. 'What does the S stand for? Stupid outerwear?'

'Woah again!' Liam struts over, trying to be cool, and hitting his head on the wind chimes. 'Are those AIRBORNE REBELLION Hi-Tops? In aquamarine?'

COOL-O-METER

SUPERCOOL

CHILLING OUT

NO SWEAT

IN THE SHADE

COLD FEET

ON THIN ICE

LUKEWARM

HOT AND BOTHERED

SWEATING BUCKETS

TOTAL MELTDOWN

'Naturally. They literally cost more than all your trainers put together,' he sneers at my canvas pumps. 'You, like, <u>CHOSE</u> to wear those? Tragic. And I mean, bare ankles used to be a thing, but now, like, totally not a thing.'

'I've got Low-Top Revolutions,' Liam fawns. 'Been waiting to upgrade forever.'

'You <u>SHOULD</u> upgrade.' He fist-bumps Liam, while staring at me. 'And not only your footwear. I'm Zac. Zac Cassidy. I own eleven pairs of trainers.'

'How many feet have you got then?' Jess rolls her eyes.

He spots the notebook in Liam's hand and snatches it.

'What's this?'

'Um, splans. Special plans,' Liam shrugs. 'We're coming up with new crisp flavour mash-ups.'

'Wait! I literally just thought of one that will blow your mind.' He nods to the gang behind him.

'This'll be good,' one of them says. 'He's awesome at everything.'

Zac cracks his knuckles and announces: 'Chineapple. Mic drop. Boom.'

'Geniosity!' Liam slaps his forehead. 'Why didn't you think of that, Stan?'

'Cheese and pineapple?' I mumble. 'How did I miss that?'

'You're not Zac Cassidy,' says one of his gang members, popping bubble gum.

'Guys, this is The Dogs,' Zac introduces them. 'This is my look-out, Tash. Always states the obvious.'

'Hi everyone!' says a girl taller than Liam, with black braided hair piled on top of her head. 'We've literally just arrived!'

'This is Mason. Doesn't say much. He's the hired muscle.'

Mason is the owner of the biggest pair of shoulders I've ever seen. It's like he's

COOL-O-METER

SUPERCOOL

CHILLING OUT

NO SWEAT

IN THE SHADE

COLD FEET

ON THIN ICE

LUKEWARM

HOT AND BOTHERED

SWEATING BUCKETS

TOTAL MELTDOWN

wearing a wardrobe. A wardrobe with a crew cut that's threateningly spinning a yo-yo while not taking his eyes off me.

'And this is Maddie, my second in command. What she doesn't know about bubble gum isn't worth knowing, eh, Mads?'

'Whevs.' She chews at us from underneath a spiky fringe, streaked with purple—the only flash of colour because she's dressed head to toe in black, including a slouched beanie.

'Now, I'd much rather be parasailing in the Caribbean, cos OMG we're in the middle of lame united.' Zac gestures around him. 'And we're not really here to be mentors, so you better be up for something more than crisp flavour mash-ups.'

'Yeah like no,' Liam tries to say casually.

'And we need something better than special plans.' He chucks my notebook back at me. 'We need SUPER-DARES, and if you do one I might let you join my gang. It's just a bit of fun.'

In my experience, whenever anyone says

IT'S JUST A BIT OF FUN, generally it's just a bit of NOT fun.

THINGS THAT WERE SOLD TO ME AS JUST A BIT OF FUN BUT I WANT MY FUN MONEY BACK:

1. Equations
2. Having a pen pal
3. Looking after your brother
4. Courgette fairy cakes
5. Flip-flops
6. Doughnuts without jam
7. Holding a stick insect
8. Weeding
9. Goalkeeping
10. Mazes

Oh, and

11. Dares

'Coolamundo, cos I do dares ALL the time,' Liam fibs.

'Decent. You can start by chucking the wind chimes on the fire.'

COOL-O-METER

SUPERCOOL

CHILLING OUT

NO SWEAT

IN THE SHADE

COLD FEET

ON THIN ICE

LUKEWARM

HOT AND BOTHERED

SWEATING BUCKETS

TOTAL MELTDOWN

Liam freezes to the spot, suddenly aware of what a super-dare is.

'PEEEEEEEP!'

Luckily Petra interrupts with a whistle.

'S'up guys!' she says, hi-fiving everyone. 'This is my magical children herder. Anytime I blow this you pay attention, yeah? Now you probably don't realize it yet, but Whispering Woods is one of the Seven Wonders of the World.'

Some of Fred's **SEVEN WONDERS OF THE WORLD** include **BIG BEN**, **WOTSITS**, and **SKIPPING**. By the look on his face Whispering Woods isn't going to be joining them.

'I spy with my inner eye . . .' Petra pushes her red glasses up her nose and studies us. 'A hedgehog—prickly, but soft on the inside.'

She points to Maddie, who hides beneath her spiky fringe.

'And a fox—able to overcome challenges, with the mind of a survivor.'

She winks at Idris and he instantly agrees.

'Or perhaps a sheep—never questioning authority and preferring the safety of numbers.' She clicks her fingers at Flossie, and I'm pretty sure she's got that one wrong.

'Excuse me, I'm a unicorn,' Flossie pouts.

'I'm deffolo a sloth,' Liam yawns. 'Give me a hammock and I'm sorted.'

'Well, let's birds-eye-view that for a minute.' Petra steps back. 'The sloth is indeed the world's slowest mammal. So slow that algae has time to grow upon it.'

Liam checks the back of his hoodie.

'Sloths have such weak legs, they pull themselves along on their bellies.'

'Oh, I totally do that reaching for the remote control.'

'And they can turn their heads almost full circle.'

Liam tries to turn his head further than is good for him until Petra turns it back.

'But you are totally NOT a sloth.'

Fred is huffing and puffing and on the verge of exploding. I try to reach for my

COOL-O-METER

SUPERCOOL

CHILLING OUT

NO SWEAT

IN THE SHADE

COLD FEET

ON THIN ICE

LUKEWARM

HOT AND BOTHERED

SWEATING BUCKETS

TOTAL MELTDOWN

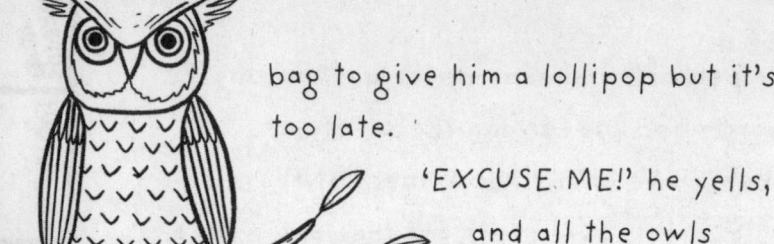

bag to give him a lollipop but it's
too late.

'EXCUSE ME!' he yells,
and all the owls
probably die of heart
attacks. 'WHEN ARE WE
DANGLING FROM JELLY-HOPTERS AND
EATING TRANCHLAS?'

'One thing I can promise is you'll eat
a gut-load of marshmallows,' Petra says.
'Organic ones obvs. But you'll have marshmallows for legs by the time you leave.'

'Flint Danger doesn't have time for legs;
he's too busy looking for trouble.' Fred
takes out two loo rolls taped together.
'That's why I brung my nocklears.'

Rufus appears with his ukulele,
strumming it to punctuate his speech.

'There are wild animals out in the woods
this very minute . . . the tiny wood mouse
who can shed his tail if he's caught . . . the
pipistrelle bat who can gobble up three
thousand insects a night . . .'

'And the elephant hawk moth who can see colour in the dead of night,' interrupts Zac.

'Nice,' Rufus nods. 'You didn't get GENIUS OF THE TERM for nothing.'

'I've got a phobia of moths,' Jess says. 'It's called Mottephobia.'

'I've got a phobia of Zac,' I say under my breath.

'I've got a phobia of woods in the dead of night that might be full of zombies,' Liam adds. 'It's called dead-of-night-wood-zombie phobia.'

'That's not a thing,' Jess tuts.

'There's nothing to be afraid of here, pufflings,' Petra says. 'Just . . . don't go near the farmer's land. There are things in that field no old crow wishes to see.'

'What? Like, werewolves?' Liam gulps.

'No. Scarecrows, obviously.'

Flossie shrieks, and spies through her magnifying glass into the trees.

'My big bruvver Orson

COOL-O-METER

SUPERCOOL

CHILLING OUT

NO SWEAT

IN THE SHADE

COLD FEET

ON THIN ICE

LUKEWARM

HOT AND BOTHERED

SWEATING BUCKETS

TOTAL MELTDOWN

came here a long time ago, and told me about the scarecrows. He said they come to life and steal your fings one by one. Then one dark night . . .' She pauses to put the magnifying glass up to her mouth so it enlarges her teeth way more than necessary, '. . . they come for your brains!'

All the small-year-olds gasp.

'You've heard the stories?' Rufus says. 'Who knows what tinkles the chimes and rustles the leaves . . . maybe it's the wind, or maybe—'

'It *is* the wind,' Mr Fisher tuts, having finally set up his tent. 'We didn't come here for *silly* nonsense.'

'Well I came here to drink my own pee.' Fred folds his arms. 'And I'm not leaving till I do.'

WHEN IT'S ACCEPTABLE TO DRINK YOUR OWN PEE

☐ Whenever the need arises

■ Never in a bajillion years

'I can drink more pee than you!' comes a boast I never thought I'd hear, as a Larkfield small-year-old with a bunch of freckles stomps around the camp and squares up to Fred.

I automatically go into protective older brother mode, which means staring at her disapprovingly from a safe distance.

'Who even *ARE* you?' Flossie puts her hands on her hips.

'Billie Keegan.' She flicks her plaits. 'The bestest at everything, so nur.'

'Are you really? Cos don't make me put a lie test on you.'

'Hey kids, enough of the pee talk!' Rufus empties his cup on the fire. 'It's time to switch on your magical light tubes and head bedward. Tomorrow we're up at early o'clock—when the hunt for our inner animals begins.'

Everyone turns on their torches and makes their way to the Slumber Shacks. The

COOL-O-METER

SUPERCOOL

CHILLING OUT

NO SWEAT

IN THE SHADE

COLD FEET

ON THIN ICE

LUKEWARM

HOT AND BOTHERED

SWEATING BUCKETS

TOTAL MELTDOWN

parent helpers seem
particularly keen to finally
be turning in.

'Are there really tiny
meeces who lose their tails?'
Fred grabs my hand.
'And scary scarecrows?'

'It's ok Fred, there's
nothing to worry ab—'

'Cos that's BRILLIANT!'
he shouts, in no way
frightened at all.

'Right, well if you do need
me, use this.' I hand him the
map of camp, to which I've
made a few amendments.
Though I realize it might be
me needing him.

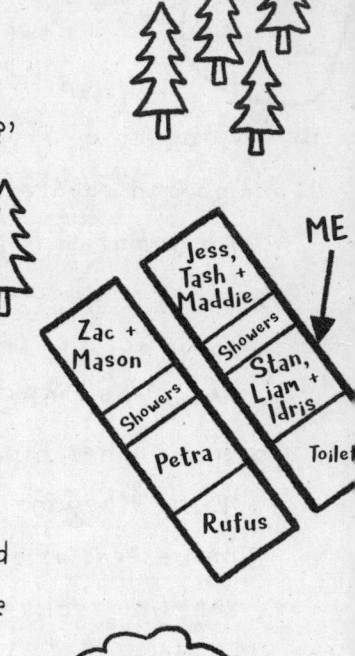

READING TREE

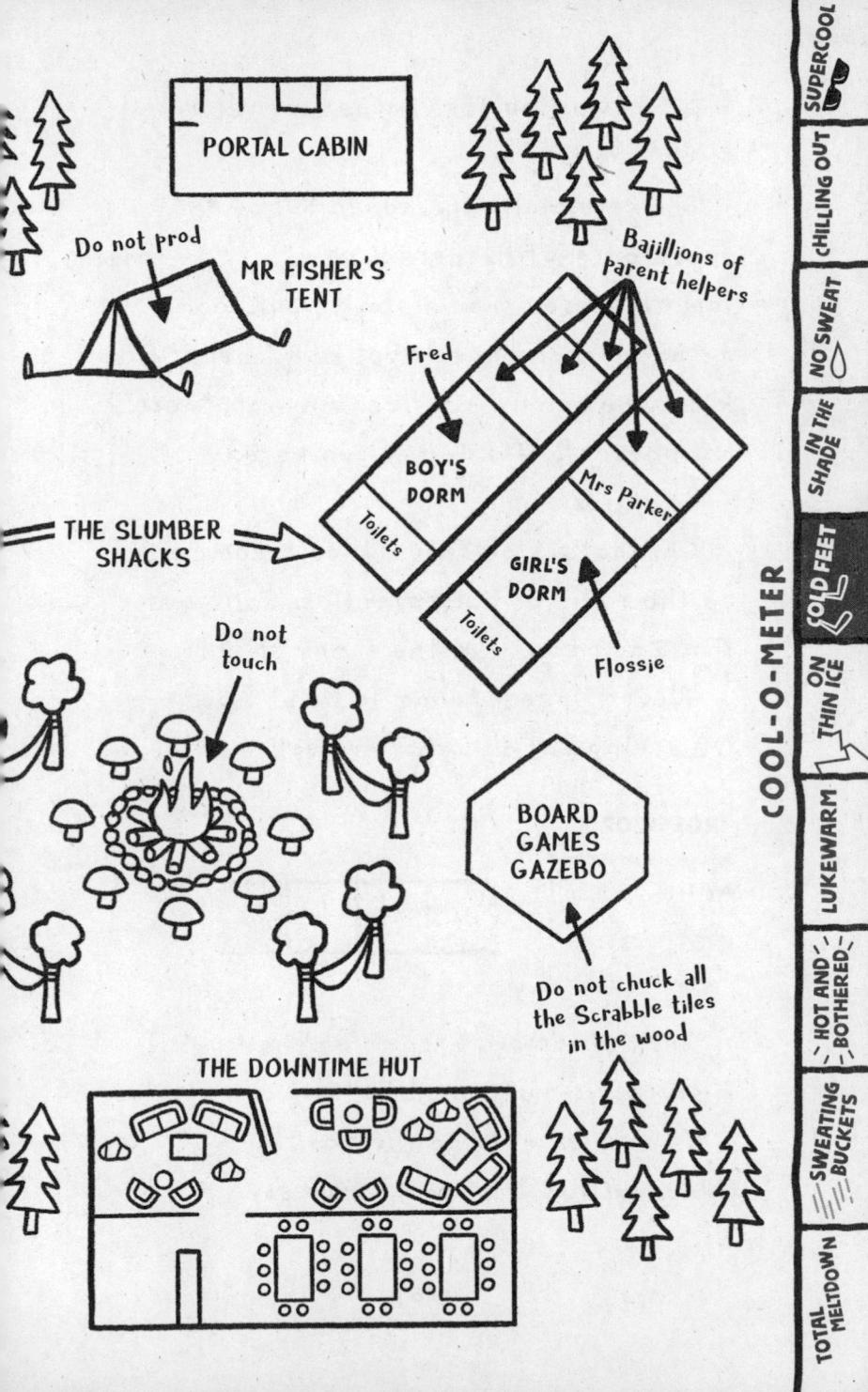

Zac is waiting for us when we return to our room.

'See you totally chickened out of the super-dare. Still, there'll be plenty of time tomorrow. You should stay in our room; me and Mason haven't got <u>BABY</u> beds.' He kicks the bunk I'm sat on. 'Anyway, there's an indecently funny smell in here.'

He stares at me.

'Oh, that's Stan's musty ice cream socks on the radiator,' Liam replies, oblivious that Zac means I'M the funny smell.

If ever I needed Liam to be blivious, it's seeing Zac for what he really is:

CROSSWORD

ACROSS
1. Git (3)

'Until tomorrow, frenemies!' he laughs, flicking his quiff and strutting out.

'This is going to be the most **MAGNIFULOUS** trip ever,' Liam says, as we scoff Gran's brownies.

'Um, yeah, definitely,' I say, hoping not too many of our splans involve Zac Cassidy, and I note Idris catches my gaze.

'I've totally got scarecrow phobia though,' Liam says. 'And Mr-Fisher's-livid-purple-beetroot-face phobia.'

'We definitely haven't got cake phobia.'

'Now THESE,' Idris mumbles with a mouthful of cake, 'are one of the Seven Wonders of the World.'

'Mmm-hmm.' And then we spit it out at the same time, because Mum has snuck some of her revolting pea brownies in too.

'PEAS IN CAKE?' Liam cries, wiping his tongue on the duvet. 'That is illegal, man-bro! We should claim for false advertising.'

We have to eat loads of snacks to make up for it.

RECIPE FOR DISASTER
* Brownies
* Peas
Only mix if you want to traumatize everyone for life

SUPERCOOL

CHILLING OUT

NO SWEAT

IN THE SHADE

COLD FEET

THIN ICE

COOL-O-METER

LUKEWARM

HOT AND BOTHERED

SWEATING BUCKETS

TOTAL MELTDOWN

 # STICKS AND STONES

Mercury's egg-shaped orbit means it sometimes has a double sunrise. One sunrise is <u>MORE</u> than enough at Whispering Woods.

'Red sky in the morning, shepherd's yawning.' Fred grabs my hand and makes us skip to breakfast.

Rufus wasn't joking about being up at early o'clock. I've already had to make eight beds, tie six shoelaces, and help Fred with his latest Flint Danger accessory.

'REMEMBER!' Flint Danger shouts, while flying a hot-air balloon into a hurricane. '*THE KEY TO SURVIVAL IS <u>ALWAYS</u> <u>AVOID DEATH!</u> THAT'S WHY I WEAR MY FLINT DANGER SURVIVAL BUM-BAG—*

FILLED WITH EVERYTHING I NEED NOT TO DIE'.

Well, we'll be all right if we need an emergency ration of Jammie Dodgers—that's all Fred's got in his. Unfortunately, I need more than biscuits to help me stay awake, having been up most of the night after eating pea brownies. Every time I eat one of Mum's vegetable-filled monstrosities I end up with cake nightmares and indigestion.

WORST EVER CAKE NIGHTMARES

The one where a wizard visits my house and tells me I've got to lead a band of misfits across a rugged continent to throw a courgette fairy cake into a volcano

The one where I wake up over the rainbow and can only get home if I eat the sweet potato muffin

The one where apes have taken over the Earth and eaten all the food except parsnip sponge cake, which is the reason all the humans died in the first place

The one where Fred and Chewbacca fly off in the Millennium Falcon, abandoning me on a beetroot cake planet

COOL-O-METER

SUPERCOOL
CHILLING OUT
NO SWEAT
IN THE SHADE
COLD FEET
ON THIN ICE
LUKEWARM
HOT AND BOTHERED
SWEATING BUCKETS
TOTAL MELTDOWN

There's no chance of a hearty breakfast either. We're on serving duty under the watchful eye of Mrs Fry, the campsite cook, with instructions not to eat all the organic bacon.

'How come Larkfield get the cushy job of setting tables?' Idris says dishing up sausages as everyone shuffles past the serving hatch.

'Hey, you can't complain—whatever we drop is ours, right?' Liam flings two rashers on the floor before scoffing them. 'Zac gave me the tip.'

He's been talking about Zac non-stop since we woke up.

'Right, mentors,' Mrs Parker says, having jumped ahead of the queue. 'We're due a win against Larkfield—the **GREAT BIG SCHOOL CHALLENGE** is ours for the taking. All you need to do is remember everything they teach you.'

'But that sounds like school, Miss.'

'That is the general idea, Liam,' she tuts

and moves along to me. 'Can I have a quick word, Stan?'

'I've been expecting this,' I say, serving her a poached egg. 'Fred's been feeling homesick hasn't he? Don't worry—I'm fully prepared with my **FRED ALERT KIT**.'

'Oh no. He's made himself *very* at home, along with a fair amount of invertebrates,' she sighs, closing her eyes for a moment. 'Quite traumatic to wake up to snails <u>ALL OVER</u> the dormitory. Can you encourage him to keep them outside?'

'Yes, course. Sorry.'

She waltzes off, and Fred's up next.

'This would be the bestest day of my entire life if I didn't have to eat yuck.'

'Flint Danger eats yuck. Barbecued tarantulas, remember?'

'It's my PUDDING tummy that's empty.'

'Mine too.' Flossie screws her nose up, pulls out a packet of strawberry laces and starts sharing them out.

'Gimme one!' Billie Keegan demands.

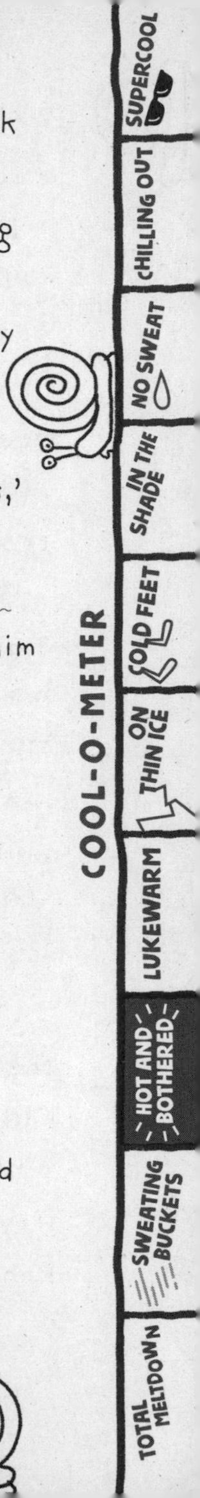

Running vertical sidebar (COOL-O-METER):

COOL-O-METER
- SUPERCOOL
- CHILLING OUT
- NO SWEAT
- IN THE SHADE
- COLD FEET
- ON THIN ICE
- LUKEWARM
- HOT AND BOTHERED
- SWEATING BUCKETS
- TOTAL MELTDOWN

'That's not how you ask for fings AT ALL.' Flossie hides the packet.

Billie stomps off, flicking her plaits at us.

'Does she stomp EVERYWHERE she goes?' I ask.

'She's Maddie's sister, and she chews everywhere SHE goes,' Jess moans. 'Even in her sleep. She could seriously do with reading up on How to Be a Roommate.'

'Billie Keegan's still not as annoying as Stan.' Flossie scowls at me, taking out an ink pad from her rucksack. 'I need your fingerprints, buster! My favourite unicorn hat has gone missing and you were the last person to touch my suitcase!'

'You think I took it? I'm already sorted in the ridiculous hat department, thanks.'

I've made sure to stuff my bobble hat at the back of the wardrobe in the hope it'll fall into Narnia.

'We can do this the easy way, or the hard way,' she says, refusing to move. Before I know it, I've splodged my fingerprints in her notebook.

'Be thankful you don't live with her,' Jess says. 'She interrogated us for five weeks when someone ate the last Jaffa cake.'

Not all the organic bacon in the world can make up for having to do star jumps with Mr Fisher.

'Come on, mentors! It's a beautiful spring day, and this'll get the circulation going!' he wheezes. 'We're out nature walking, and that requires stamina.'

'I did NOT sign up for this.' Liam gets a stitch and leans against a tree.

'What splans do you fancy?' I ask, jumping up and down. 'How about my What Kind of Cake Are You questionnaire?'

'Oh, sorry Stan, I'm on probation today. Zac wants to see if I've got what it takes to join The Dogs.'

I stop suddenly.

'And what DOES it take?'

COOL-O-METER

SUPERCOOL

CHILLING OUT

NO SWEAT

IN THE SHADE

COLD FEET

ON THIN ICE

LUKEWARM

HOT AND BOTHERED

SWEATING BUCKETS

TOTAL MELTDOWN

'He says we should be able to cause havoc at a moment's notice.' He gets out a bag of Hula Hoops. 'Super-dares are the new splans, mate-bro—it's on-the-spot chaos.'

It brings me out in a cold sweat thinking about it. No one can spontaneously come up with a quiz about cake. It takes careful planning on two sheets of A4.

'Zac once wore his shirt back to front for a laugh. He caused a fashion sensation in Larkfield that lasted *FOUR TERMS*.' Liam whistles. 'See? That's what I'm talking about.'

I once wore my pants back to front, but all I caused was a great deal of discomfort. I realize Zac and I are never going to meet in a Venn diagram.

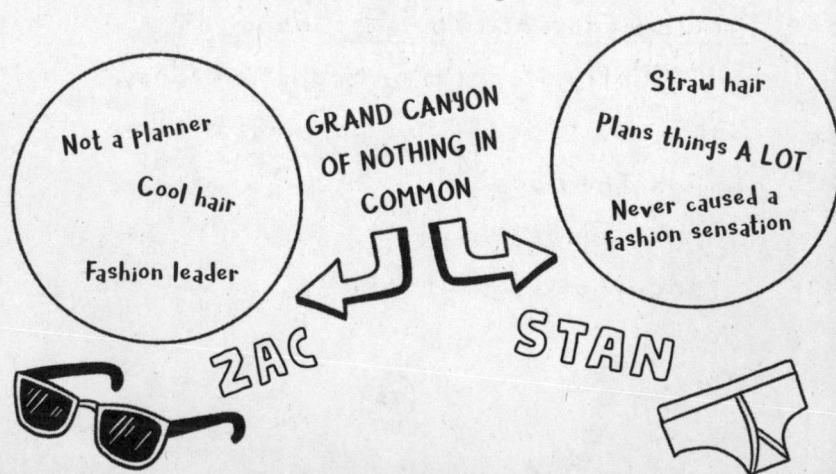

Not a planner

Cool hair

Fashion leader

GRAND CANYON OF NOTHING IN COMMON

Straw hair

Plans things A LOT

Never caused a fashion sensation

ZAC

STAN

'Liam Miller! Are you eating again?' Mr Fisher's face is already quite far up his angry scale, which may be due to the star jumps. 'Come here and give me ten!'

'Oh, but Sir—'

'Postpone those thoughts, Norman,' Petra calls over. 'For the brain needs a workout too. Liam, come here and give me ten . . . bird species—go!'

'Erm . . .' Liam shoves the Hula Hoops in his back pocket. 'Man blackbird, lady blackbird, man robin, lady robin, hawk of prey—'

'What do they teach you at that school?' She holds up her hand as Mr Fisher blushes. 'Here's two for free—over there you've got your chaffinch. It's a male; you can tell by the pink colouring. On the branch a nuthatch. See its distinctive black eye-stripe, like a bandit?'

'Isn't that a bullfinch, Petra?' Zac swaggers in with his gang, and points to another bird.

'Sure is, Zachary. You'll be winning

COOL-O-METER

SUPERCOOL

CHILLING OUT

NO SWEAT

IN THE SHADE

COLD FEET

ON THIN ICE

LUKEWARM

HOT AND BOTHERED

SWEATING BUCKETS

TOTAL MELTDOWN

Mentor of the Day at this rate.' She high-fives him.

'Keep 'em sweet and they don't suspect you of anything,' he whispers to Liam, who immediately leans back to admire Zac's hiking boots. 'These are my top-of-the-range Earth Whisperers. Built for hard-core terrain with outstanding grip and shock absorbers.'

I didn't realize we were supposed to pack FOUR-WHEEL-DRIVE shoes. Though if I were wearing them right now I'd drive myself out of here—Rufus has just made a startling announcement involving clip-on fox tails.

'Hey mentors, get ready to hop on the happiness train! When I call your name, grab a tail—that way the little ones will LITERALLY be able to hang out with you. Zachary Cassidy, you're up first!'

'Can't wait to help, Rufus.' Zac smiles, then turns around to The Dogs. 'Lame united. Ditching this first chance I get.'

'CAN I HAVE NATASHA PEMBERTON, MASON DONOVAN, IDRIS PHILLIPS...'

'Zac's so cool,' Liam dreams aloud. 'He's got a gaming chair with vibration feedback AND cupholders.'

'MADDIE KEEGAN, LIAM MILLER, STANLEY FOX...'

'He's even got a hot tub with hydro-massage bubble jets.'

'We've got one of those,' I reply, clipping on a tail. 'As long as you don't mind sharing a bath with Fred.'

'AND FINALLY CAN I HAVE ALASKA MCGREGOR.'

'Who?' We all look around.

'Isn't that in the Arctic, Rufus?' Zac asks.

'It's what I've got written down here. Alaska McGregor.'

'There's nobody here with that name,' I say. Until I realize there's somebody here with that SURNAME. I turn around and there, with a face so hot it could melt lead, is Jess.

COOL-O-METER

SUPERCOOL

CHILLING OUT

NO SWEAT

IN THE SHADE

COLD FEET

ON THIN ICE

LUKEWARM

HOT AND BOTHERED

SWEATING BUCKETS

TOTAL MELTDOWN

'I'm going to <u>KILL</u> whoever's responsible for this,' she says through clenched teeth and walks straight up to Rufus. 'I prefer to be called Jess.'

'Too bad.' He makes a note. 'If I were called Alaska, I'd dress in fake furs and really sell it.'

'ALASKA?' sniggers Maddie as Jess walks past. 'Well, that doesn't surprise me. It always gets chilly when you walk in our room.'

Zac gives her a fist bump.

I try to catch up with Jess but she's too far ahead in the happiness train as we follow a pathway that runs next to the farmer's land. That's when I spot them— the scarecrows, sat in the middle of the ploughed field with their sack faces and button eyes looking menacingly in my direction as their flappy clothes flap in the breeze. Thankfully we take a sharp left into the woods. The warmth of the sun doesn't reach us, so I pull on a jumper that now comes with added mint choc chip stains.

'Jess! Wait up!' I call after her, dragging some small-year-olds by my tail.

'Not surprised you need a jumper,' Maddie laughs. 'You're getting closer to Alaska!'

'You'd never catch me in a jumper with stains on it,' Zac sneers.

'Hush pufflings!' Petra beckons us beneath a canopy of trees, pushing her glasses up her nose. 'I spy with my inner eye . . . a zebra! Striking appearance and happiest in a group.'

She points to a boy in a stripy top, who quickly hides behind his friends.

'And here's a kangaroo—bit jumpy, and strongly protective of younger offspring,' she says, pointing to me.

'Oh, and an owl—a wise head on young shoulders.'

'I AM SO MUCH MORE THAN AN OWL,' Jess says under her breath.

'Maybe some of you are deer. Shy,

COOL-O-METER

SUPERCOOL

CHILLING OUT

NO SWEAT

IN THE SHADE

COLD FEET

ON THIN ICE

LUKEWARM

HOT AND BOTHERED

SWEATING BUCKETS

TOTAL MELTDOWN

unpredictable, like hanging out in small herds, and licking your noses to help your sense of smell.'

Flossie tries to touch her nose with her tongue.

'Let's deer the situation,' Petra says, cupping her hands over her ears. 'Deer ears move in different directions, always listening out for danger. Close your eyes and draw a map in your mind of all the things you can hear.'

I'm not sure any of the places on my mind map belong in a wood:

Fred huffing: 'Flint Danger eats deers on toast for breakfast.'

Zac whispering: 'Lame united, time for super-dares.'

Tash commenting: 'So woods are, like, just a bunch of trees, yeah?'

Jess mumbling: 'Owl? If anything I'm an Atlantic Puffin.'

'Jess . . .' I tip-toe over to her. 'What's all this Alaska business?'

'Can we not discuss it while everyone's got deer ears!' she hisses, as faces turn towards us.

'Personally I'd <u>LOVE</u> an amazesome name, like Maverick or Cornwall,' Liam sighs.

'My mum knew a Jebediah and a Zebediah at the actual same time,' Tash says, ducking under a branch. 'That's like the same name but different capital letters.'

'Can we change the subject?' Jess snaps.

'Easy Alaska, you might cause an avalanche!'

Maddie earns another fist bump from Zac.

'EXCUSE ME!' yells Fred, and everyone instantly regrets having deer ears.
'FLINT DANGER WOULD HAVE CLIMBED VOLCANOES BY NOW IN JUST HIS PANTS.'

'Hey, focus your audio, little fella.' Rufus ruffles his hair, immune to the fact Fred's hair mainly smells of wet donkey.

He stamps his foot, takes out Angus and feeds him a leaf.

'Woah, he's a beauty!'

COOL-O-METER

SUPERCOOL

CHILLING OUT

NO SWEAT

IN THE SHADE

COLD FEET

ON THIN ICE

LUKEWARM

HOT AND BOTHERED

SWEATING BUCKETS

TOTAL MELTDOWN

'He's Angus,' Fred pouts.

'Well, Angus here has over 14,000 teeth, which he uses to scrape up his food. Want to know another snail fact?'

Fred shrugs, pretending he doesn't care.

'Think snails are harmless to everything but lettuce?' Rufus leans in. 'Cos the cone snail is one of the deadliest creatures on the planet. He hides in coral reefs, biding his time . . . until he fires a harpoon at his prey, paralysing his victim and reeling it in before—GULP! He swallows it whole!'

Fred's mouth is about as wide as it can go—Rufus has him hooked like a venomous cone snail. He beckons us all over to a muddy puddle where he scoops his fingers into the mud and wipes it on his cheeks.

'If I was a badger, I'd get through hundreds of worms in one night.'

'Are we eating worms?' Fred almost bursts with excitement.

'Tempting though it is, no.' Rufus tucks leaves in his beard. 'Badgers have an excellent sense of smell, like most animals in this wood. To stand a chance of seeing anything we need to blend in with our surroundings organically.'

Fred is already five steps ahead, having laid down and rolled through the ENTIRE puddle, because one of Flint Danger's best friends is camouflage. Tash shrieks as she wipes a bit on her chin and sticks fern in her braids.

'I mean, it's a bit gross, but also totally a bit fun.'

Liam pokes fern in his hair like rabbit ears, and the parent helpers join in too as we hold tails and weave in and out of the trees.

'You wouldn't catch me smelling like the wood,' Zac sneers. 'I sprayed on Giovani Donatello's RUGGED this morning. It's already got undertones of bark and moss.'

'Yeah, no, ridiculous.' Tash wipes it off, followed by Mason and Liam, as they realize it's a lame thing to do because Zac says so. They return to their STUPID

COOL-O-METER

SUPERCOOL

CHILLING OUT

NO SWEAT

IN THE SHADE

COLD FEET

ON THIN ICE

LUKEWARM

HOT AND BOTHERED

SWEATING BUCKETS

TOTAL MELTDOWN

dares, which involves chucking sticks at trees so raindrops fall on everyone's heads.

'Oh look,' Maddie grins, having got a perfect shot above Jess. 'It's raining in Alaska.'

Jess shoves past her and drags me behind a tree.

'If you've got a pie chart on how to erase everything that's just happened,' she whispers, 'now would be a good time to hand it over, Stan.'

'Distraction's always good. You could point out my middle name's Winston. And not after a great-grandfather or anything sensible like that.'

'At least that name's normal for HUMAN BEINGS. Did you think with a brother called Orson and a sister called Flossie, I was just plain Jess?'

'There's nothing plain about—'

'And that's not the worst of it. Why stop at one silly name when you can have

THREE? I mean, did they ever think I'd become prime minister? *YES, PRIME MINISTER ALASKA, OF COURSE WE'LL TAKE YOU SERIOUSLY, said NO ONE EVER ON THE UN SECURITY COUNCIL!'*

Her voice echoes around the wood, and a squirrel freezes for a moment before scurrying off again.

'*THREE?*'

She drags me closer, before checking no-one's listening with deer ears. 'You're not to breathe a word of this to anyone. Promise?'

The only promises I've ever broken involve Fred and things that should be left outside in the garden to eat Dad's lettuces.

'Promise.'

'Oh God, I can't believe I'm telling you . . .'

COOL-O-METER

SUPERCOOL
CHILLING OUT
NO SWEAT
IN THE SHADE
COLD FEET
ON THIN ICE
LUKEWARM
HOT AND BOTHERED
SWEATING BUCKETS
TOTAL MELTDOWN

⮑ THE DARE

Plenty of things have unexpected names.
Especially in space. Take the rocks on
MARS called Space Ghost, Nibbles,
Warthog, and Nigel.

That still doesn't prepare me for what
Jess has said.

'You what?'

'I said,' and she pulls at blades of grass
to accentuate every word, 'my name is
Alaska. Pixie. Lemondrop. McGregor.'

'Woah . . .' I say, taking a while to digest
it. 'That's . . . nice.'

'Only if you're a chihuahua.' She grabs a
stick and snaps it in two. 'Unbelievably, it
could have been worse. If I'd have been a
boy they were going to call me Aslan.
Would have put me off Narnia for life.'

'That would have been ROAR-some

though . . .'

She glares at me, and I add it to the list of **WHEN NOT TO MAKE A JOKE:**

When Mr Fisher reaches Vivid Purple Beetroot.

When Mum accidentally puts Fred's snails through the wash.

When Idris can't find Wi-Fi.

And when your friend reveals her alarming real names.

'My Gran was called Jess. I stayed with her when my parents went to find themselves on organic farms in Cambodia. When they came back, I refused to answer to anything else. Luckily they believed in free will and harmony. But my real name is on UNDERLINE. Including school trip medical forms.'

'No one will care after tomorrow, you'll see.'

Suddenly we hear a twig snap and spot

SUPERCOOL
CHILLING OUT
NO SWEAT
IN THE SHADE
COLD FEET
ON THIN ICE
COOL-O-METER
LUKEWARM
HOT AND BOTHERED
SWEATING BUCKETS
TOTAL MELTDOWN

Maddie running out from behind a tree.

'They will when I find out the rest of your stupid names, Alaska!' she says, flapping her deer ears, then takes great pleasure in yelling across the wood that Jess's inner animal must be a penguin.

'Actually penguins only live in the SOUTHERN HEMISPHERE,' I shout back, finally able to use one of Flint Danger's facts.

'Yeah, well I'm gonna look up some stuff about Alaska and you're going to wish you lived there—ice queen!'

'If only I WAS an ice queen, I'd freeze her into an ice cube and watch her slowly melt over crocodile-infested waters,' Jess hisses, and part of me wishes she was an ice queen too, although another part of me is glad she isn't because I haven't returned some of her books.

Thankfully Maddie's near the rear of the happiness train as we head deeper into the wood. Petra tries to get us to tune into our

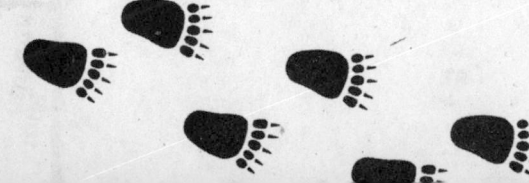

senses to track animals, like butterflies who taste with their feet. 'And that's kinda what we should be doing, pufflings. Make every step count, and travel with care.'

I can see Fred about to explode with his outdoor voice again, but I'm too far away to shove the harmonica in his gob.

'EXCUSE ME!' he shouts, and all the worms bury to Australia. 'FLINT DANGER SAYS THERE'S ONLY ONE WAY TO TRAVEL, AND THAT'S ROLY-POLYING.'

It's true that Flint Danger spends 90% of his time drop-rolling across all five continents, which Fred is demonstrating.

'Woah!' Rufus says. 'You'll flatten all the wildlife, dude.'

'It needs to be flattened.'

'You wouldn't say that if you met the purple bubble raft snail . . .'

Fred stands up and frowns at Rufus with his Why face.

'Not only does it have a beaut of a violet shell, but it spends its whole life

SUPERCOOL

CHILLING OUT

NO SWEAT

IN THE SHADE

COLD FEET

ON THIN ICE

COOL-O-METER

LUKEWARM

HOT AND BOTHERED

SWEATING BUCKETS

TOTAL MELTDOWN

floating upside down with a homemade raft of bubbles. This snail doesn't eat lettuce, either. It eats the most <u>DEADLY JELLYFISH IN THE SEA</u>. And get this, it starts off as a male, and becomes female. Cool, huh?'

Fred looks gobsmacked and a little teary. 'I didn't fink I could love snails more.'

'Exactly. Now let's harness that positivity and maybe tiptoe like a fox. If you check out these footprints you can see he walks on his toes like a stealthy ninja. You can tell a lot from the tracks an animal leaves behind.'

You can tell a lot from Fred's too—anytime you're in a hurry, Fred will slow you down.

Hopping

TRACKING FRED

Lost dinosaur
slippers

Dinosaur
slippers

Distracted
by a snail

Being a lion

Star jumps

Walking backwards

Out of puff

COOL-O-METER

SUPERCOOL

CHILLING OUT

NO SWEAT

IN THE SHADE

COLD FEET

ON THIN ICE

LUKEWARM

HOT AND BOTHERED

SWEATING BUCKETS

TOTAL MELTDOWN

While the parent helpers join in
with being foxes, I watch Liam fake
laugh at Zac's jokes and try to casually
lean against trees. I can't help thinking
of Neptune's moon Triton, which is slowly
falling towards it, getting closer and closer
until eventually it will be ripped apart.

'Looks like he's got what it takes to be
in The Dogs,' Idris notes. 'What you need is

Me giving him a piggyback
all the way home

to build a campaign with a hashtag. It's the way to go with anything these days. I can help. All I need is ten minutes, access to Wi-Fi, and a Kit Kat.'

'What are you going on about?'

'Saving your bromance. It's all about Zac and Liam since we got here. Or Ziam as I like to call them.'

Everything's fine, I tell myself as I hear Ziam's echoing laughter at anyone who doesn't own eleven pairs of trainers.

'I know what'll cheer us up,' Idris says. 'Cake. The trouble with being in the woods is there's no snack cupboard . . . until now!'

He unzips his coat to reveal a tremendous array of inside pockets.

'Welcome to my jacket cupboard! Mum made me some serious pocket alterations—I've got fairy cakes, biscuits, and bacon.'

'Bacon?' Jess frowns.

'Nicked it from the breakfast buffet.' He takes out a couple of rashers. 'Bit fluffy, but still tasty.'

It's the greatest invention I've ever seen. We hide in a hollowed tree scoffing most of his jacket stash. Unfortunately, Mr Fisher is an expert at sniffing out pupils eating illegal snacks and is about to give us a punishment of ten push-ups, until Petra interrupts.

'Let's reboot those brains instead—give me ten . . . trees. Go.'

'Um . . . tall tree?' Idris looks around for inspiration.

'Er . . . conker tree?' Jess shrugs.

'Do hedges count?' I ask, as if I know ten different types of hedge.

'Willow! Oak! Cherry! Beech!' shouts Zac the tree-swot.

'Knew I could rely on you.' Petra smiles. 'Maybe take a leaf out of Zachary's books, and level-up your knowledge. There are ancient oaks in this wood that lived through the Spanish Armada, silver birch whose wispy branches were tied into witches broomsticks, and yew trees whose poison will stop your very heart.'

We only ever see one side of the Moon—
it takes the same amount of time to turn on
its axis as it does to orbit the Earth, so the
dark side is always hidden from view. Just
like Zac's dark side is always hidden from
teachers. It makes me want to find a yew
tree and brew a potion.

Instead we spend the afternoon building
giant birds' nests so we can 'appreciate the
amazing structures of our little feathered
friends.' Personally I could have done
without Rufus telling Fred about swiftlets,
which construct their nests entirely from
gloopy saliva.

'You'd never catch me building a giant
bird's nest made from spit.' Zac turns his
nose up as I sit in the middle of it. No. Zac
gets his cronies to build his while he lazes in
a tree, and still manages to get all the credit.

As we make our way back to the cabins,
he keeps pulling everyone's tails until
Petra and Rufus look over and he instantly

switches to Swot Mode.

'That's, like, literally a robin,' he points.

Idris tries to take my mind off it by filming his documentary, when suddenly Maddie lets out a scream.

'Who did that? I bet it was <u>YOU</u>, Alaska!'

Someone has just fired a lump of mud at her leg.

'I had nothing to do with it!' she protests from behind me. 'And my name's Jess!'

'I saw you.' Zac shrugs. 'I hate telling on anyone, but it's my moral responsibility.'

'No you didn't!'

'Um, I saw you too,' Liam mumbles, looking at his trainers.

'Oh dear,' Mr Fisher tuts, leaning over and grabbing a catapult stuffed in Jess's hood. 'Make your way to the kitchens, Miss McGregor. Tell Mrs Fry I've sent you to help.'

She runs off, and I can't help thinking Zac's behind all this. To top it off, he gets a Mentor of the Day sticker.

COOL-O-METER

SUPERCOOL

CHILLING OUT

NO SWEAT

IN THE SHADE

COLD FEET

ON THIN ICE

LUKEWARM

HOT AND BOTHERED

SWEATING BUCKETS

TOTAL MELTDOWN

'You officially won the wood today, Zachary,' Rufus winks.

'Just cos he knows what a bullfinch is,' Idris says as Zac walks past, swiping nettles with a stick.

'I'm naturally brilliant,' he smirks.

Pyrite is naturally brilliant. It's a mineral that sparkles with pretty golden crystals. It's also known as fool's gold, because people often think that's what it is. But it's worthless and gives off a smell like rotten eggs.

He's not fooling me.

⮑ REVENGE OR NOT REVENGE

There's not much that can't be fixed with cake. Unfortunately, at teatime there <u>IS</u> no cake. The only pudding is fruit. Which is why the dining hall is empty apart from Fred hiding under a table.

'I'm not coming out till the 'scusting narnas go away,' he sulks, pulling down the tablecloth, where he's set up camp with his Jammie Dodgers.

It seems an ideal time to work on my secret project, so I crawl under with him. I open the encyclopaedia I've borrowed from the book exchange, and start scribbling in my notebook.

97

COOL-O-METER

SUPERCOOL
CHILLING OUT
NO SWEAT
IN THE SHADE
COLD FEET
ON THIN ICE
LUKEWARM
HOT AND BOTHERED
SWEATING BUCKETS
TOTAL MELTDOWN

Polar bears

Northern Lights

Over 130 volcanoes

ALASKA

It's illegal to wake a sleeping bear to take its photograph

Fond of stone circles

P

Magic

Mischievous

Sweet

Lemony

Melt like troubles high above chimney tops

Someone whips back the tablecloth. It's Flossie, who scrambles under too.

'My favourite unicorn socks have gone missing and I'm on the lookout for justice,' she says, studying my feet through her magnifying glass. 'What's your shoe size, punk?'

'It's none of your business.'

'It is my business, and pretty soon you'll be singing like a canary.'

I go to make my escape, until I spot Zac's designer trainers walking into the room. He's whispering to Tash, so I feed Fred and Flossie biscuits to keep them quiet.

'We're all set for tonight,' Zac whispers. 'I've got loads of supplies. It was decently easy.'

'You're such a complete genius!' Tash says. 'Can't wait for DOG DISOBEDIENCE CLASS, when we can be, like, disobedient.'

'And M-Dog—remember to be on door duty at nine o'clock. Don't let anyone in our room who's not cool. It'll be proper legendary.'

Mason grunts as he spins his yo-yo. I'm convinced they can hear my heart beating.

'I've invited Liam,' Zac says. 'We need to start planning an immense super-dare for him to do on the last night of camp—he's stupid enough to do anything I tell him.'

They walk off. Finally I breathe out.

COOL-O-METER

SUPERCOOL

CHILLING OUT

NO SWEAT

IN THE SHADE

COLD FEET

ON THIN ICE

LUKEWARM

HOT AND BOTHERED

SWEATING BUCKETS

TOTAL MELTDOWN

Once the coast is clear, I crawl out and head to the kitchens to look for Jess.

'She went off in that direction, love.' Mrs Fry points a spatula towards the woods.

I've never seen a tree like it—it looks like an octopus, if an octopus were made of bark and didn't need to live under the sea. Jess is nestled in one of the low-hanging arms that twist from the bulging belly of the trunk.

'Nice reading tree,' I say, climbing up beside her.

'Depends who's in it.'

'I'd have been mad too, by the way, if I had a bonkers real name, and everyone kept going on about it all day long, and I happened to have a catapult.'

'I didn't do it, Stan.' She puts down her book. 'It's like a game of Guess Who? Once I've eliminated all the suspects, Zac's the only one left standing. He set me up. Besides, I wouldn't have aimed at Maddie's leg.'

'Fair point. Anyway, I've got something to show—'

'Hey guys! I've been looking for you,'
Idris interrupts, climbing up between us.
'I made a film of Fred today for your mum,
watch this.'

He starts the video on his phone.

*IDRIS VOICEOVER: 'HERE
IN THE MOUNTAINS OF PERU, WE
FIND FRED DANGER ON ANOTHER
INTREPID EXPEDITION.'*

The camera pans round and zooms in
on Fred, picking his nose.

*'I'M FRED DANGER. I BEEN
IN THE JUNGLE FOR TOOTY-SIX
MONTHS. I'M AS HOT AS LAVA.'*
He wipes his brow. *'TO SURVIVE IN
THE WILD YOU HAVE TO LIVE ON
THE HEDGE.'*

SUPERCOO
CHILLING OUT
NO SWEAT
IN THE SHADE
COLD FEET
THIN ON ICE
COOL-O-METER
LUKEWARM
HOT AND BOTHERED
SWEATING BUCKETS
TOTAL MELTDOWN

He karate chops the air then spots
something on the ground and picks up a worm.

'IF I WAS A BADGER, I'D
GOBBLE THIS UP AND EAT A
BAJILLION MORE.'

Unbelievably he tries to lick it, but
thinks better of it.

'I'm sure Mum will love it.' I roll my eyes.

'It hasn't finished. Keep watching.'

The camera zooms out, and I notice
someone hiding behind a tree. Someone
with leaves stuck in his hair like rabbit
ears. It's Liam with a catapult, ready to
aim, and when he fires, a scream is heard
in the distance. 'WHO DID THAT? I BET
IT WAS YOU, ALASKA!'

'It was Liam!' Jess sits up. 'And he
blamed it on me.'

'I don't believe it . . .' I stare at the
paused screen.

'He's gone over to the dark side and no

mistake,' Idris says.

'This is brilliant; we've got proof!' Jess jumps down. 'Let's take it to Fisher.'

'Um, we HAVEN'T got proof,' Idris jumps down too.

'But—you just saw it.'

'We take this to Fisher, and he'll confiscate my phone before we've had a chance to collect REAL proof. It wasn't only Liam, was it?'

'Idris is right,' I say. 'Zac's behind all this. If anything we need to help Liam before he ends up in real trouble. Zac's planning a super-dare for the last night, and wants him to do it.'

'I might've known you'd stick up for him. Liam has got a brain.' She hesitates, realizing what she's said. 'Actually, yeah, he needs our help.'

'So what are we going to do?' Idris asks, opening his jacket and offering us the last of his bacon, which I decline politely, seeing as it's been in there at body temperature since breakfast.

SUPERCOOL
CHILLING OUT
NO SWEAT
IN THE SHADE
COLD FEET
ON THIN ICE
LUKEWARM
HOT AND BOTHERED
SWEATING BUCKETS
TOTAL MELTDOWN

COOL-O-METER

There's a pause. And I realize I know exactly what to do.

'I'm going to a Dog Disobedience Class,' I announce.

'A what?'

'I'm not EXACTLY sure. But there's a chance I can find out about the super-dare. Oh, and we have until nine o'clock to make me cool.'

'Three hours?' Idris gasps. 'We're not miracle workers, Stan!'

I could easily take offence. Three hours may seem like ages, however, as Mum always says, 'TIME FALLS DOWN A RABBIT HOLE OF CHAOS WHEN YOU HAVE CHILDREN'. As demonstrated in my EGG-TIMER EGG-SPERIMENT OF FRED:

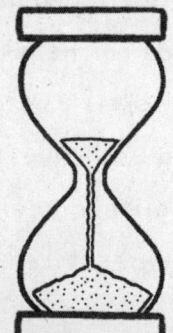

Putting socks on:
Twenty-five minutes
(excludes flinging interval)

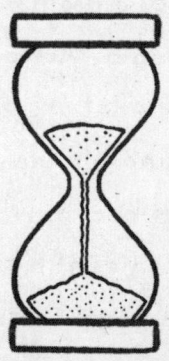

Finishing sprouts on
Christmas Day: Boxing
Day afternoon

Leaving the house
to visit Auntie Julie:
Anything up to a week

Going to bed: A
never-ending eternity
of mayhem

COOL-O-METER

SUPER

CHILLING OUT

NO SWEAT

IN THE
SHADE

COLD FEET

THIN ICE
ON

LUKEWARM

HOT AND
BOTHERED

SWEATING
BUCKETS

TOTAL
MELTDOWN

'Actually, it's less than three hours.
Mrs Parker's volunteered me to read a
bedtime story, and that could go on until—'

'—the world ends,' Jess finishes my
sentence, her eyes glazing over, as if
remembering the last story she read to Flossie.

'Go, Stan,' Idris says. 'Meet us back at
the room as soon as you can. It's time to
call in the Style Crew.'

They're already running off into the
distance. Part of me feels a pang of pride
at my mates' enthusiasm to help out. Until I
realize it's panic in trying to make me cool.

'This better be a scary story, buddy, cos I've about had it with my fings going missing.'

Flossie's now lost her unicorn face masks, which means her and Fred can't play 'trotting unicorns' any more.

'Are you sure you packed all this stuff?'

She glares at me. I grab a book as a group of them surround me in the dormitory and I begin to tell them a story about a mouse who walks through a wood.

'That's not scary,' Flossie interrupts, and the rest seem to agree as they fold their arms in protest. 'Just TELL us one.'

'I don't know any!'

'Do I have to do everyfing myself round here?' she harrumphs, climbing onto a chair and switching on a torch. 'Get comfy, amigos. This is called . . . **THE SCARECROW WOT ATE EVERYONE'S BRAINS**.'

By the time she's finished, we're all wide-eyed, perched on the edge of the beds, and I'm sat hugging a pillow.

'Again! Again!' they all chant.

'Um, I think that's enough stories about murderous scarecrows. Time for bed.'

I call in the back-up of the parent helpers and scarper, keen not to hear any more of Flossie's tales. As scary things go, it's pretty much up there with Fred's bogie collection.

MOST DISTURBING
THINGS BAR CHART

COOL-O-METER

SUPERCOOL
CHILLING OUT
NO SWEAT
IN THE SHADE
COLD FEET
ON THIN ICE
LUKEWARM
HOT AND BOTHERED
SWEATING BUCKETS
TOTAL MELTDOWN

As I walk back to the dorms I bump into
Mrs Parker.

'Get yourself up Scrambly Hill, Stan,
there's a stargazing session going on.'

I check my watch. Seeing as I'm out
quicker than planned, I've got time.

'If you want to be a sky-watcher, it's
good to know where the North Star is,'
Petra says as I reach the top of the hill.
'Have you found it yet, Norman?'

'Um . . . that bright one?' he
frowns through the telescope.

'That's Venus, with more volcanoes than
any planet in the solar system.' She points
a laser pen at it.

'Yes, of course,' Fisher coughs. 'I was
just testing.'

'The best way to find the North Star is to
find the Plough,' Petra says.

'Oh, that's my favourite constellation,' Mr
Fisher grins.

'Um, it's not a constellation,
Sir,' I say. 'It's an asterism—

a pattern of stars in the sky—that's part of
the Great Bear. I know because, well, it's
on my face.'

I point to the seven freckles on my right
cheek. Fred joined the dots once while I
was taking a nap on the sofa. It took three
days for the pen to wash off.

Petra takes a closer look.

'Ooh, now on Stan's face, the Plough's
two outer stars form an imaginary line all
the way to his nostrils, where nobody really
wants to go!'

She laughs for way more than necessary.

'But in the sky, they point to the North
Star.' She shows the way with the laser.
'And once you've found it, you're sorted.
Unless you're in the southern hemisphere,
and that's a whole different kettle of stars.'

'Or you could check out the map on your
phone,' Zac says, wandering up the hill.
'The lame stars can't point the way to the

COOL-O-METER

SUPERCOOL

CHILLING OUT

NO SWEAT

IN THE SHADE

COLD FEET

ON THIN ICE

LUKEWARM

HOT AND BOTHERED

SWEATING BUCKETS

TOTAL MELTDOWN

sweet shop, can they?'

'Kids don't know how to do anything without their mobiles,' Mr Fisher tuts.

'That is totally literally well not true,' says Zac.

By the time it's my turn on the telescope, clouds have covered most of the sky.

'I was hoping to spot the ORION NEBULA,' I sigh.

'Yawnsome.' Zac grabs the telescope. 'I mean, you can't see aliens or nothin'.'

He points it down and focuses on the horizon.

'That's more like it! Panic over everyone—I've found a sweet shop!'

I look through too and spot a big sweet sign. The only place there are MILKY WAYS tonight.

⤷ REBUILDING STAN

It can take millions of years for some species to evolve into better forms of themselves. I've got twenty minutes.

'You're late.' Idris ushers me into our room where Jess has set up a flip-chart she's borrowed from the Portal Cabin.

'*IS THAT SERIOUSLY WHAT WE'VE GOT TO WORK WITH?*' comes a voice from Idris's phone.

He's set up a group video chat with his brother Zeke and two of his friends, who are staring disapprovingly at the lost property box that's been dumped on my bed.

'Come on guys, I thought you could make fashion from anything—that's what you always boast about,' Idris tuts. 'Stan, meet the Style

COOL-O-METER

SUPERCOOL
CHILLING OUT
NO SWEAT
IN THE SHADE
COLD FEET
ON THIN ICE
LUKEWARM
HOT AND BOTHERED
SWEATING BUCKETS
TOTAL MELTDOWN

Crew—Zeke, Ash, and Lola. Together they have the capability to build the world's first Cool Stan. Isn't that right, guys?'

'ONLY IF YOU GIVE US A BUDGET AND A TWO-WEEK TURNAROUND, BRO.'

'The last time I checked we were in the middle of the woods, BRO. This is all I have, and we need something RIGHT NOW,' Idris says. 'We just have to find the gems amongst the not gems.'

'THERE AIN'T NO GEMS IN THERE, BRO.'

'NO. GERMS ARE WHAT YOU'VE GOT IN THERE.'

'NICE ONE ASH.'

They all laugh.

'Surely what I'm already wearing is better than what's in there?' I shrug.

'YEAH, YOU BETTER TIP OUT THE BOX,' Zeke says, with no confidence in my outfit. 'SHOW US ANYTHING WITH A PRINT.'

'AND HIT ME WITH ACCESSORIES, PEOPLE.' Lola clicks her fingers.

Between them they come up with a FIVE

POINT PLAN TO A COOL STAN which Jess writes up on the flip-chart.

---

* Hair that comes from the
21st century

* Clothes that look like you didn't
think about them but you sooo did

* Nonchalant shrugging

* Confidence that owns the
furniture when you walk in a room

* Some well-placed accessories to
take you from fool to cool

I don't like to tell them we're going to fall at the first hurdle, unless they're used to working with hay for hair.

'I'm sensing a montage!' Idris shouts over Zeke's music blaring from his phone.

You know those cool montages they have in movies where the zero trains to be a hero, normally in a warehouse filled with chains and tyres? This is nothing like that.

COOL-O-METER

SUPERCOOL

CHILLING OUT

NO SWEAT

IN THE SHADE

COLD FEET

ON THIN ICE

LUKEWARM

HOT AND BOTHERED

SWEATING BUCKETS

TOTAL MELTDOWN

I have no dignity left as they size up my feet, my haircut, and elbows. Clothes fly everywhere as Idris and Jess take orders from the Style Crew.

'ROLL THOSE CUFFS! CHOP THE HEM!'

'LOSE THE MITTENS, BRO, THAT IS NOT WHAT I MEANT BY RETRO.'

'WE'VE GOT TO DO SOMETHING ABOUT THE HAIR. YOU GOT A SLOUCHED BEANIE IN THERE SOMEWHERE?'

'This is the closest thing we've got, Lola,' Jess says, throwing me a hat.

It's a beret.

'MM-KAY. MAYBE TRY AND ROCK A EUROPEAN VIBE, STAN?'

I reluctantly look in the mirror and hardly recognize myself in the cobbled together nightmare:

☆ T-shirt featuring Kermit the Frog
☆ Beaded necklace wrapped around my wrist four times
☆ Unbuttoned checked shirt with

rolled-up sleeves to cover what I hope
is ketchup
☆ Jeans with more hole than jean
☆ Sunglasses that are actually shaped
like flowers
☆ An odd pair of trainers (one too
big, one too small, both needing a
tetanus jab)
☆ Bow tie
☆ Beret definitely not rocking a
European vibe

'I know what you're thinking,' Idris says.
'Who's this amazing fella, right?'

I'm thinking who is this <u>NOT</u> amazing
fella, as I turn sideways in the mirror
hoping a different angle is all my outfit
needs. I look like one of the scarecrows.

'Why am I wearing different trainers?'

'A DIFFERENT-PAIR-OF-TRAINERS IS
THE NEW SAME-PAIR-OF-TRAINERS,' Zeke
says. 'I'VE ALREADY SET UP A HASHTAG.'

'Hold your breath,' Idris says, spraying

COOL-O-METER

SUPERCOOL

CHILLING OUT

NO SWEAT

IN THE SHADE

COLD FEET

ON THIN ICE

LUKEWARM

HOT AND BOTHERED

SWEATING BUCKETS

TOTAL MELTDOWN

me all over with DYNAMIC ICE PITS. I cough from beneath the fug of deodorant.

Suddenly there are noises in the corridor. It's Ziam and The Dogs heading to Dog Disobedience HQ. I gulp.

'Stan, you can do this.' Idris grabs my shoulders. 'Just the cool saunter to master, c'mon.'

I strut up and down the room, slightly limping on one side, swinging an arm, and tripping up on my different-sized trainers. I'm the missing link of humankind's evolution.

'LET'S HOPE YOU'RE MOSTLY SITTING DOWN,' Zeke says. 'GOOD LUCK DUDE!'

Idris hangs up the call as Jess hands me bubble gum she's nicked from Maddie's drawer.

'Remember, Stan, lose the charts.' She takes my notebook. 'You need to be like them.'

'Well, I was hoping it

116

wouldn't come to this,' I say, ripping a page out of it. 'Glossary of Liam words. From the early days when I was trying to understand him. Brillendous or what?'

I take a deep breath, walk down the corridor to Zac and Mason's room, and knock on the door. I feel my head spinning, making a weird whirring noise, but realize it's Mason's yo-yo as he opens the door. For a moment he doesn't recognize me. Then he grunts and mumbles:

'You're not allowed in.'

He goes to shut the door until I shove the larger of my trainers inside, which luckily is more trainer than toe: 'I think we need to ask Zac-a-doodle-do. Mate-bro.'

'Woah!' Zac walks over, and takes off his shades as he looks me up and down. 'You're an explosion of clothes that shouldn't have happened.'

'I sort of like it though,' Tash says over his shoulder. 'In a totally-literally-shouldn't-like-it type way.'

COOL-O-METER

SUPERCOOL

CHILLING OUT

NO SWEAT

IN THE SHADE

COLD FEET

ON THIN ICE

LUKEWARM

HOT AND BOTHERED

SWEATING BUCKETS

TOTAL MELTDOWN

'And the trainers, two different kinds?' Zac raises an eyebrow as they discuss me.

'So you can wear your faves in one go.' Tash shrugs. 'I mean, is that genius or not?'

'Yeah, well totally literally I'm ahead of my time,' I interrupt, shoving my way into the room and shrugging nonchalantly. Amazingly Zac steps aside. I strut in, swinging one of my arms, chewing gum, trying to act like I own the curtains. 'I'm here for the Dog Dis-obedience Class. Whatever.'

'As long as you promise to keep your charts to yourself,' Zac says.

'Obvs. Lame united.'

'Come and help yourself to the artisan buffet!' Tash leads me to a table full of food. 'We've got fruit preserves, smoked cheeses, and sourdough baguettes.'

'Wowington,' I say, lifting up my flowery sunglasses. 'Where did all this come from?'

'Benefits of sleeping in a room away from annoying adults.' Zac taps his nose. 'Not only can we stay up all night, but I can sneak out and get into the kitchens. The stupid cook leaves the window unlocked.'

'Cool, cos I'm starvacious.' I grab a plateful and check out the room. It's bigger than ours, with proper beds, and duvets that look as if they're made from clouds. There's even an outdoor patio area with a lovely view of the woods.

'Find a seat—film's about to start.'

All the bed space is taken by Maddie and, mostly, Mason's shoulders. I spot Liam on a beanbag, and strut across trying not to trip over my feet.

'You look . . . different,' he frowns. 'Wait a minute, since when did you wear a bow tie? And where'd you get that hat from?'

'I'm doing casual, mate-bro.' I squeeze in behind him. 'So, what's all this about?'

'Disobedience class—a chance to break some rules. Zac's hacked into the camp Wi-Fi. He's such a genius. Hey, are you wearing two different trainers?'

COOL-O-METER

SUPERCOOL
CHILLING OUT
NO SWEAT
IN THE SHADE
COLD FEET
ON THIN ICE
LUKEWARM
HOT AND BOTHERED
SWEATING BUCKETS
TOTAL MELTDOWN

119

'Never mind that. What's the film?'

'It's part of my initiation. I've officially joined The Dogs once I've watched this. The other part was absolutely disgusti- nating, but I can't tell you any more. The first rule of The Dogs is not to talk about The Dogs—and that's the second, third and fourth rule too.'

'Dogs!' Zac interrupts. 'You're gonna love this. It's the scariest film I've ever seen, especially the surprise at the end. And if you don't watch it, you're all scaredy-cat-babies. Especially you, L-Dog.'

Immediately I'm regretting my life choices when it starts with a zombie limping through the woods and most of the food is teenagers. Now I realize why he's making Liam watch it.

I cross my fingers, hoping Mr Fisher will walk in on us and give us all reflection sheets for illegally using Wi-Fi. I might not have my notebook, but it still doesn't stop me drawing up a cake chart in my mind.

TIMES I'VE WISHED A PORTAL WOULD OPEN UP BENEATH ME

When I played Idris's video game that actually did require a portal to open up beneath me, but I got incinerated by the dragon instead

When Mr Fisher walked in the classroom carrying the same planet-themed rucksack as me

When Liam and Idris caught me on the ladybird ride with Fred at the fair, and OK, I might have been enjoying myself a bit too much

When Auntie Julie reminded everyone I wet my pants aged seven, because I refused to go to her toilet in the basement next to a boiler that sounds like an axe-wielding maniac

COOL-O-METER

SUPERCOOL

CHILLING OUT

NO SWEAT

IN THE SHADE

COLD FEET

ON THIN ICE

LUKEWARM

HOT AND BOTHERED

SWEATING BUCKETS

TOTAL MELTDOWN

⤷ WHITE DWARF

'Never have I been more grateful for Liam's tallness, because I mostly watched his shoulders,' I explain to Jess as we clear the breakfast tables.

Although I was also grateful for Liam's tallness on a day trip to Weymouth—he's the first point of contact for bird plop.

'The film was brillendous,' he fibs. 'Even though it was ALL MY PHOBIAS in one.'

'It was **NOT** brillendous,' I say, wiping the tablecloth. 'Especially the surprise at the end.'

'What was the surprise?' Jess asks. 'Zombie come back to life?'

'Sort of.' I shiver at the memory. 'The film ended, we all got back into bed, then Zac jumped up at the window wearing a zombie mask. I'm not ashamed to say a bit of wee came out.'

'He's just pushing boundaries,' Liam says. 'It's what all the world's best geniuses do. Y'know, like Einstein and Leonardo DiCaprio. Like, this morning he told me bare ankles are back in again. Anyhoodle, gotta go, he's asked me to warm his seat in the Portal Cabin.'

If there was an Olympic event for being oblivious, Liam would have a gold medal.

'Zac is a MAJOR twerp,' Jess says as Liam walks off. 'And I've worked out what game he's playing—Jenga, so he can undermine you all and you fall at his mercy. Did you manage to find anything out about the super-dare?'

'No. But he's offered me a place in The Dogs if I do a dare today. I'm so close to gaining his trust, and then I'm sure he'll tell me everything. Amazingly, I think the outfit worked.'

I've carried my evening look to daytime. Although Idris can't believe I've ditched

COOL-O-METER

SUPERCOOL

CHILLING OUT

NO SWEAT

IN THE SHADE

COLD FEET

THIN ON ICE

LUKEWARM

HOT AND BOTHERED

SWEATING BUCKETS

TOTAL MELTDOWN

the different-pair-of-trainers trend
before it had a chance to take off, because
I've gone back to my trusty canvas pumps.

Jess grabs her rucksack.

'You sure you still want to do this, Stan?'

'I've got no choice. I have to save Liam
before he crashes into Neptune—I mean,
before it's too late.'

'You better take these.' She hands me
a bag of strawberry laces. 'I overheard
Maddie say they're his favourites. Never
know when you might need them.'

'Thanks.'

'C'mon,' Idris says. 'Fisher's teaching us
the water cycle again, and we're already
five minutes late.'

He's finally got his way on a classroom
catch-up so our brains 'don't fall to mush
out of school hours'.

I meet Fred on the way to his outdoor
lesson, swinging a jam jar. He's borrowed
one of Flossie's hair bobbles and tied his
wayward curls into one big one on top of

his head.

'It's my Flint Danger man bun,' he says. 'I can do just about anyfing now.'

It's true that Flint Danger has faced many a dangerous situation, as he reminds us in one of his adverts:

BEING FLINT DANGER IS A PERILOUS BUSINESS. SOMETIMES I'VE EVEN HAD TO AMPUTATE MY OWN HAIR, WHICH IS WHY I ALWAYS SECURE IT IN A FLINT DANGER MAN BUN HAIR WRANGLER, PRICED £15.99

'Stupid rain lessons.' He scuffs his feet on the gravel. 'I should be arm-wrestling lions.'

'Hang on a minute, it didn't rain last night, Fred. How come your jam jar's full? And with really quite yellowy rain that's got a good head of froth on top . . .'

He shrugs.

COOL-O-METER

SUPERCOO...

CHILLING OUT

NO SWEAT

IN THE SHADE

COLD FEET

ON THIN ICE

LUKEWARM

HOT AND BOTHERED

SWEATING BUCKETS

TOTAL MELTDOWN

'Please don't tell me that's—'

'It's special sparkly rain that fell from the twinkly stars.'

'It's wee, isn't it?'

'Billie Keegan filled hers with wee too,' he pouts. 'And I can drink it when I get thirsty.'

'No absolute way you're ever doing that,' I say and make him tip it away.

'Remember, children, indoor voices and marshmallow footsteps,' Mrs Parker shushes, as she herds them to the outdoor classroom.

'EVEN IN THE OUTSIDE, MISS?' Fred hollers.

'Especially in the outside. The farmer's across the way, and he's allergic to children.' Mrs Parker pulls me to one side. 'Can I have a quick word, Stanley?'

'Sure. Need to make use of my **FRED ALERT HOMESICK KIT**?'

'Again, quite the opposite. He went to bed in full camouflage last night. Could you remind him that leaves, mud and worms are *NOT* pyjamas.' She takes a deep breath. 'What with Flossie and her missing items, I'm absolutely certain I'm not paid enough.'

Right on cue Flossie walks by, studying me through her magnifying glass, which enlarges her eye and makes me feel *VERY* uncomfortable.

'You fink you're a tough guy, doncha? Who you working for, the CIA?'

'Floss, I'm innocent. I mean, I don't even like unicorns that much.'

She gasps.

'That does it!' She takes out her handcuffs. 'You have the right to remain *silent*—'

Luckily a parent helper drags her away before she can arrest me.

There's no sign of Fisher as I sit next to Liam and nudge him awake.

'I am completely full of no beans,' he yawns.

'Where are your Hula Hoops?'

SUPERCOOL
CHILLING OUT
NO SWEAT
IN THE SHADE
COLD FEET
COOL-O-METER
ON THIN ICE
LUKEWARM
HOT AND BOTHERED
SWEATING BUCKETS
TOTAL MELTDOWN

'Zac wanted to share them.'

By 'share' he means scoff the whole packet himself as he super-dares Maddie to draw an unflattering picture of Mr Fisher on the flip chart.

'Places, everyone!' Tash rushes in, having been on look-out. 'He's literally behind me!'

'Brrrrr!' Maddie laughs, sitting down in front of Jess. 'Did someone leave the fridge open? Oh no, my mistake, it's just the largest US state sitting in our classroom.'

Zac high-fives her.

'Bore off, Maddie,' Jess snaps, as Mr Fisher stumbles in, bumping into a table. He's as sleep-deprived as Liam.

'Did you not sleep, Norman?' Zac asks in his fake concerned voice.

'That may be how you do things at Larkfield, Mr Cassidy, but in my classroom it's Mr Fisher to you.'

He spots the drawing and amazingly just flips the page without saying a word.

'What with the sheep bleating endlessly

in the upper field, the cockerel with his infernal alarm call, and the endless tinkle of wind chimes, you tend to wake a little earlier.' He takes a big gulp of coffee. 'Right, flow-chart time!'

Everyone groans, except obviously me, as he hands out activity sheets with instructions to draw up the water cycle. Zac finishes his in a few minutes and asks if he can get Mr Fisher another coffee.

'No thank you, Mr Cassidy, but I appreciate the offer.'

I can't believe Fisher is falling for his charms. I finish my work and pull the sheet from underneath Liam's slumped head.

'Let me help you . . . woah! What's this?'

He's drawn a MASSIVE flow chart. Liam's never drawn a chart voluntarily in his ENTIRE LIFE.

COOL-O-METER

SUPERCOOL
CHILLING OUT
NO SWEAT
IN THE SHADE
COLD FEET
THIN ICE
LUKEWARM
HOT AND BOTHERED
SWEATING BUCKETS
TOTAL MELTDOWN

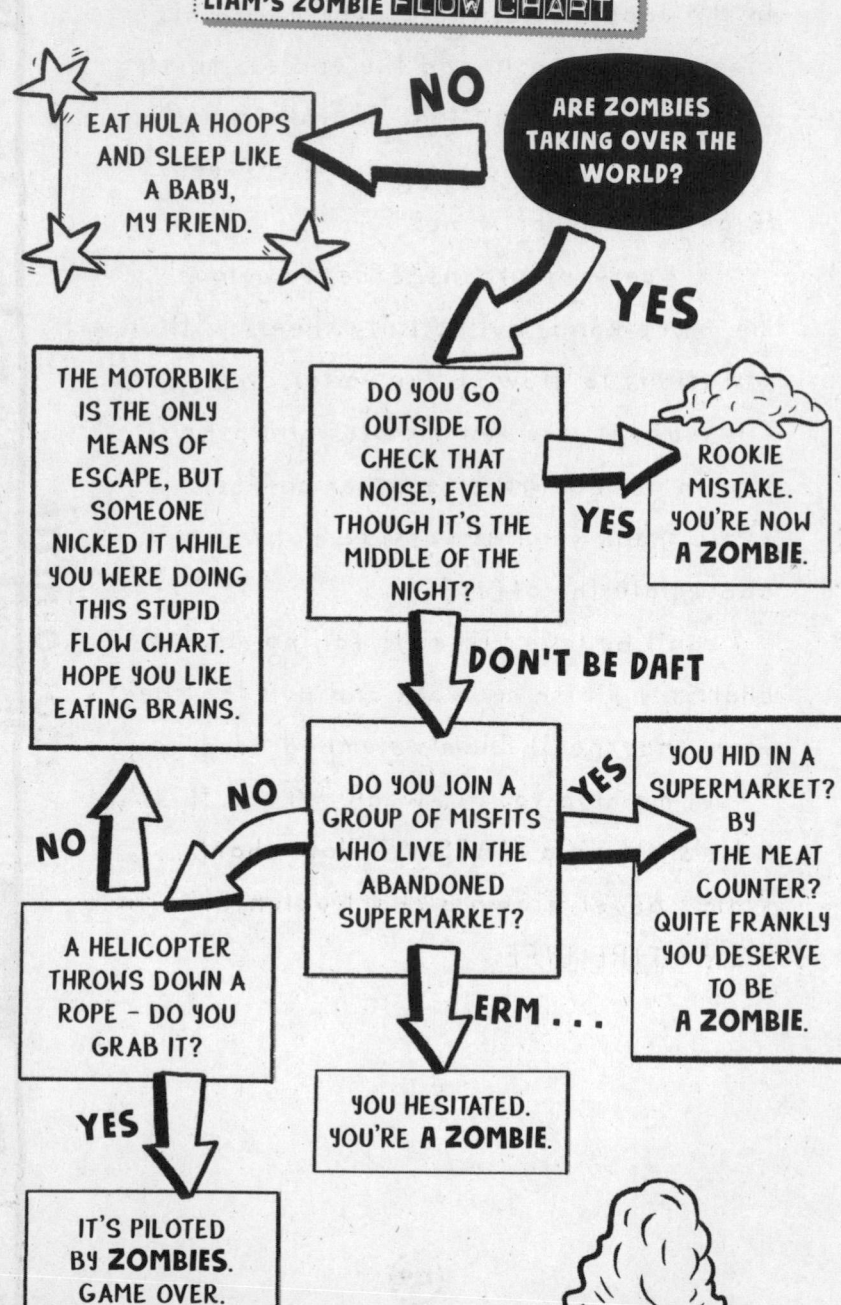

'LIAM MILLER!' booms Mr Fisher, standing over us and glowing Cherry Blush. 'Remind me, I seem to have forgotten. Did I ask you to flow-chart a zombie apocalypse?'

'Erm . . . I don't think so, Sir.'

'*NO DEFINITELY NOT, SIR*, is the right answer! Stay behind and fill it in properly.'

He orders me to stay behind too when I point out it's quite an impressive flow chart, then marches out in his alarming shorts, taking most of the class with him.

Zac sneers as he walks past.

'What's all this extra work L-Dog? You're as bad as Chart Geek over there.'

He grabs my notebook.

'Hey! Give it back!'

But he's already flicking through it.

'Oh my God, it's worse than I thought,' he laughs, throwing it to Tash.

'You've, like, literally drawn loads of charts in a book,' she says, passing it to Mason who opens it at a page.

COOL-O-METER

SUPERCOOL
CHILLING OUT
NO SWEAT
IN THE SHADE
COLD FEET
THIN ON ICE
LUKEWARM
HOT AND BOTHERED
SWEATING BUCKETS
TOTAL MELTDOWN

'Friend or Frenemy Multiple Choice Questionnaire,' he laughs, but then starts to read it as he slowly spins the yo-yo.

1. YOUR 'FRIEND' INVITES YOU TO THEIR FANCY DRESS PARTY. WHEN YOU TURN UP AS THE PLANET JUPITER, IS EVERYONE ELSE:
   a) also dressed as Jupiter?
   b) dressed as 'Mr Fisher through the ages' including his 80's perm with pastel jacket and rolled-up sleeves?
   c) wearing cool jeans and laughing at you?

2. YOUR 'FRIEND' OFFERS TO SHARE A BOX OF CHOCOLATES. DO THEY:
   a) cut every chocolate in half so you can experience them together?
   b) suggest seeing how many chocolates you can eat using your toes?
   c) only leave you the Turkish Delight?

3. YOUR 'FRIEND' ASKS TO BORROW YOUR PENCIL CASE. DO THEY:

a) take it home and personally engrave your name on every single item?

b) start a mini sword fight with the pencils to detract from Fisher's algebra lesson?

c) throw it on the school roof, laugh at you, then say 'cheer up, it's only bants'?

Mostly a) Your friends are very thoughtful.
Mostly b) Your friends are excellent at coming up with splans. **Mostly c)** WARNING! You are in Frenemy Territory!

'Mostly C,' Mason mouths, catching the yo-yo and looking up at Zac.

'You're not s'pose to <u>READ</u> them.' He snatches it off him, and flicks the page. 'I mean who wastes their time doing a Venn diagram about biscuits that are good for dunking? And what's this—a polar bear?'

'Fancy a strawberry lace?' I leap up and thrust the sweets under his nose, taking back my notebook.

COOL-O-METER

SUPERCOOL
CHILLING OUT
NO SWEAT
IN THE SHADE
COLD FEET
ON THIN ICE
LUKEWARM
HOT AND BOTHERED
SWEATING BUCKETS
TOTAL MELTDOWN

'I'll take all of them, thanks.' He goes to walk out of the room. 'But you better get rid of that if you want to be in The Dogs.'

I chuck my notebook in the bin. As soon as he's gone I get it back out again.

'Why do we want to be in his stupid gang, Liam?'

'It's hard to explain, but, when you do a dare and actually get away with it, it's amazesome.' He gazes into space. 'Especially when you don't have time to think about it.'

'Even when one of your oldest friends gets the blame instead?' I stare at him as he blushes.

'Once you join The Dogs you get sunglasses. And Zac's promised me some Airbornes. Plus you get to know all kinds of stuff—style tips and secrets and—' He pauses. 'I've already said too much. The first rule of The Dogs is—'

'—not to talk about The Dogs, yeah, I know.'

'Don't take this the wrong way, mate-bro . . .'

He gets up and puts his finished work on Fisher's desk. 'But maybe The Dogs isn't for you.'

'What, I'm not cool enough, is that it?'

'You're just a bit . . . not spontaneous sometimes, Stan.'

He walks out.

'I can be spontaneous,' I whisper.

I flick through my notebook and land on a page: <u>TOP FIVE MOST EXCITING CRATERS ON THE MOON AND HOW TO BRING THEM UP IN CONVERSATION.</u>

Fred is **NOT** impressed to be spending the afternoon studying minibeasts, especially when he finds out that doesn't mean incy-wincy lions.

'Well that would be a-MAY-zing,' Rufus says. 'Imagine their ickle roars. But seriously, dudes, minibeasts are invertebrates, meaning they have no backbone. Can anyone give me an example?'

COOL-O-METER

SUPERCOOL

CHILLING OUT

NO SWEAT

IN THE SHADE

COLD FEET

ON THIN ICE

LUKEWARM

HOT AND BOTHERED

SWEATING BUCKETS

TOTAL MELTDOWN

ZAC, I say in my head, and so do Idris and Jess by the way we look at each other.

Fred takes Angus out of his pocket and says: 'Are snails a vertybrate?'

'Abso-yes-alutely!' Rufus nods, stroking his shell. 'Angus is also crazy clever. He can close up his shell for winter by making a door out of slime to seal him in.'

Liam's not so clever, as Mr Fisher spots him eating crisps again. He's about to give him ten sit-ups when Petra interrupts.

'Let's positive the negative with a fact situation. Liam, give me ten . . . insects. Go.'

'Um . . . buzzy things, icky things, long-legged things, jumpy things—'

'Can you be more specific?' she asks, laying out ground sheets beneath the trees.

'Woodlice!' he shouts, dragging an answer out of his brain.

'Ah! Woodlice aren't insects, but crustaceans that are related to lobsters.' Petra turns over a log to reveal them.

'They've got fourteen legs, and don't actually pee, but pass ammonia as a gas through their shells.'

'Wee gas?' Liam wrinkles his nose. 'That's wrong-a-doodle-do.'

'Retrain your brain to see the beauty in everything,' she says, pushing her glasses up her nose. 'I spy with my inner eye . . . a peacock—extravagant, intelligent, and *LOVES* to be admired.'

She nods to Zac, who runs his fingers through his hair.

'And a sparrow—highly social, resourceful, and impossible to ignore.' She points to Tash. 'Ooh, and a chameleon—trying to blend in, hiding the real you, but perhaps it's time to shed your skin.'

She winks at Mason who blushes, steps back, and immediately blends in with Mrs Parker's red T-shirt.

I wish I could blend in with my surroundings too because we have to help the small-year-olds collect things that have way more

COOL-O-METER

SUPERCOOL

CHILLING OUT

NO SWEAT

IN THE SHADE

COLD FEET

ON THIN ICE

LUKEWARM

HOT AND BOTHERED

SWEATING BUCKETS

TOTAL MELTDOWN

legs than necessary.

'Remember we're killing nothing but time, guys,' Rufus says. 'So grab yourself a magical creature vessel.'

He points to a jar which Fred soon fills—he can hardly contain his excitement at the prospect of studying creatures without backbones.

'I hope I find tranchlas.'

'Tarantulas don't usually hang out off the A420,' Rufus says. 'But did you know if they lose a leg, they can grow it back?'

'My bogies do that.'

'That's a whole lot of TMI.' Rufus pats his head.

The afternoon passes with Billie Keegan thinking it's a good idea to put ladybirds all over Flossie's cardigan with the excuse: 'I'M MAKING IT DECORATED!'

'What is wrong with that Billie Keegan?' Flossie shakes her head. 'She's all shout and no fun.'

And Zac manages to help a small-year-old

overcome his fear of creepy crawlies, for which he gets ANOTHER Mentor of the Day sticker.

'I should be a psychologist or something.'

'Well he's already half way there, being a psycho,' Jess whispers.

Fred, meanwhile, is in insect heaven.

'You've got yourself a devil's coach horse!' Petra points to his jar. 'Looks a bit like a scorpion with its bum in the air, and if he gets annoyed he'll squirt a smelly liquid out of it.'

'I wish I could do that.'

'You already do,' I remind him.

After studying far too many crawlies, Petra and Rufus instruct us to release them into the wilderness, before taking the equipment back to the Portal Cabin. I watch Fred waving off three jarfuls of woodlice. He's named every single one.

'Goodbye Alan, goodbye Keith, goodbye Barbara—'

'I think it's time for a super-dare,' Zac

COOL-O-METER

SUPERCOOL

CHILLING OUT

NO SWEAT

IN THE SHADE

COLD FEET

ON THIN ICE

LUKEWARM

HOT AND BOTHERED

SWEATING BUCKETS

TOTAL MELTDOWN

says, creeping up behind me. 'And I've thought up the perfect one . . . FOR YOU.'

'You sure Stan's right for The Dogs?' Liam frowns.

'Of course I am. Bring it on,' I say, determined to show some spontaneity, though I'd rather have twenty-four hours with a chart first.

He pulls out a jar from his leather jacket.

'Super-dare you to empty this,' he whispers. 'In Fisher's tent.'

I forget to breathe for a moment, because it's crawling with bugs.

'It's just a bit of fun. Imagine the look on Fisher's face.'

Which is exactly why I DON'T want to do it. That's a Mr Fisher Livid Purple Beetroot and a Stanley Fox expulsion from not only school but the universe.

'Fisher's tent is literally RIGHT THERE.' He shoves it in my hands. 'It'll be easy. You wanna be cool and join The Dogs, don't you?'

Yes, because then I get to find out

their secrets. But part of me also wants sunglasses and trainers too. Liam's voice echoes in my head, 'YOU'RE JUST A BIT . . . NOT SPONTANEOUS SOMETIMES, STAN.'

Almost everyone else is inside the Portal Cabin. I'm about six paces away from the tent. RECORD SCRATCH. I can't believe I'm considering it.

'Any dare but this,' I whimper. 'It's just . . . me and Fisher . . . we've got history.'

'I'll do it; I'm not scared,' Maddie grabs the jar and writes on the label ALASKA MCGREGOR.

'Hey! What are you—'

But she's already run off to the tent, unzipped it, thrown the jar inside, and run back.

'You didn't open it Mads,' Zac tuts. 'Pretty crucial that.'

'Oh. I forgot,' she shrugs, winding gum round her finger.

I don't think twice. I race towards the tent and fumble around inside. Then

SUPERCOOL

CHILLING OUT

NO SWEAT

IN THE SHADE

COLD FEET

ON THIN ICE

COOL-O-METER

LUKEWARM

HOT AND BOTHERED

SWEATING BUCKETS

TOTAL MELTDOWN

someone grabs me. Someone with angry
eyebrows and alarming shorts.

'It's not what it looks like, Mr Fisher!' I
try to hide the jar behind my back.

There's only one thing worse than being
shouted at by Mr Fisher, and that's waiting
to be shouted at by Mr Fisher, while he
slowly turns every colour of his Angry
Scale. I even have time to note the colour
variations in between.

'WHAT DOES IT LOOK LIKE, MR FOX?' he
blasts me with the hot air of his fury, and I
note that LIVID PURPLE BEETROOT is
not the limit to his facial anger. There's
one more—WHITE DWARF—the core left
behind after a star has blasted all its gas
supply into space, but still immensely hot
inside.

I look across towards Maddie and Zac, who
have conveniently disappeared. Then I look
at my feet, and realize one of them is still
inside the tent, stood on a pair of his shorts.

'I'll admit it doesn't look great.' I chew

on my lip. 'But if you give me a good five minutes, I can provide a full explanation of the facts. I was actually—'

'I haven't got time for your excuses!'

Teachers never want to listen; it's easier to blame the nearest person holding the jar full of insects. Not only do I get a reflection sheet, but the punishment of serving dinner, washing up, and worst of all, SWEEPING FRED AND FLOSSIE'S DORMITORY.

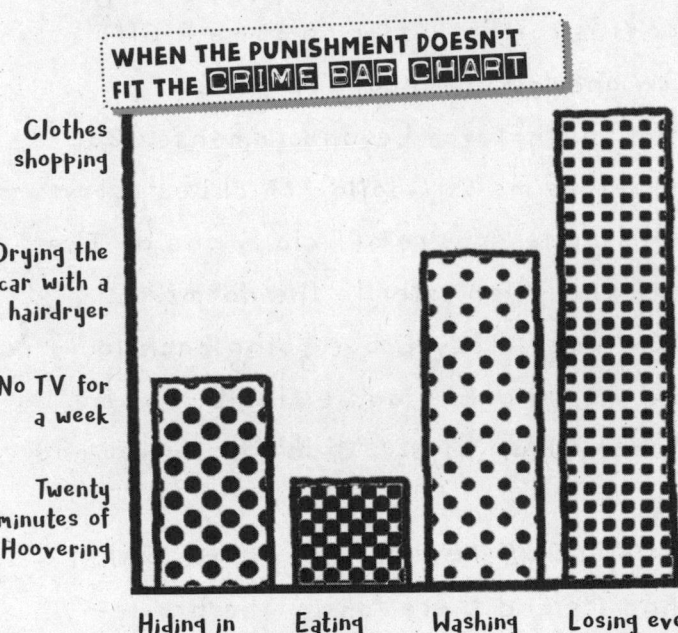

WHEN THE PUNISHMENT DOESN'T FIT THE CRIME BAR CHART

UNFAIR PUNISHMENT

- Clothes shopping
- Drying the car with a hairdryer
- No TV for a week
- Twenty minutes of Hoovering

Hiding in the cupboard when Auntie Julie comes round

Eating grated cheese on the sofa

Washing the car with the windows open

Losing every pair of gloves since the day I was born

SO-CALLED CRIME

COOL-O-METER

SUPERCOOL

CHILLING OUT

NO SWEAT

IN THE SHADE

COLD FEET

ON THIN ICE

LUKEWARM

HOT AND BOTHERED

SWEATING BUCKETS

TOTAL MELTDOWN

⤷ HAMMER STRIKE

About 600 million people gathered round their televisions to watch the Apollo 11 Moon landing in 1969. Everyone at Whispering Woods is currently staring at me RIGHT NOW and talking about Tentgate.

'S-Dog, that was beyond immense.' Zac high-fives me as I dollop chickpea curry on his plate. 'You're officially one of The Dogs. Initiation later in the dorms.'

'You were crazy-brave going back to take the lid off.' Maddie fist-bumps me.

'Woah,' Liam says. 'I didn't know you had it in you.'

EVERYONE THINKS I DID THE DARE.

And I stand there taking the praise— people are slapping me on the back

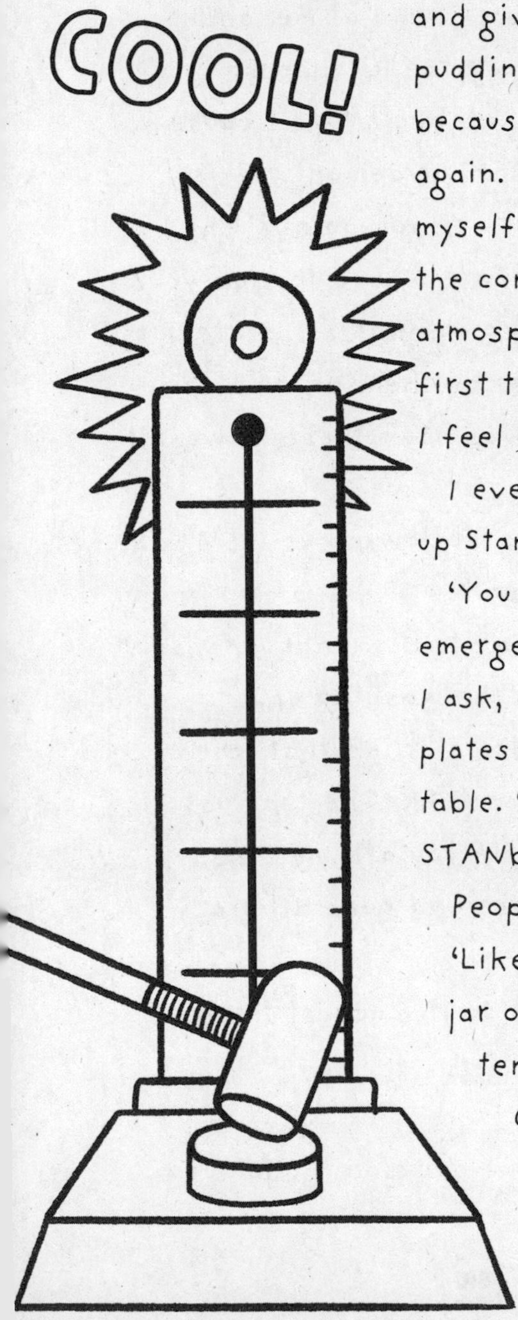

COOL!

and giving me their puddings. Or maybe because it's fruit again. But I allow myself to wallow in the congratulatory atmosphere. For the first time ever I feel COOL.

I even start making up Stan words.

'You want an emergency super-dare?' I ask, collecting up the plates from the dinner table. 'Just call the STANbulance.'

People LAUGH.

'Like, did I open a jar of bugs in your tent—or a STAN OF WORMS?'

COOL-O-METER

SUPERCOOL
CHILLING OUT
NO SWEAT
IN THE SHADE
COLD FEET
ON THIN ICE
LUKEWARM
HOT AND BOTHERED
SWEATING BUCKETS
TOTAL MELTDOWN

Jess is shaking her head at me, and dragging me towards the kitchens.

'What's that?' I call back. 'Did I cause pandemonium? No. STANdemonium.'

'Oh my God, what are you doing?' she whispers. 'Stop before I have to slap you.'

'Hey! I'm engaging in bants,' I protest, stacking the plates by the sink.

'Whatever that was back there, it wasn't bants.'

'No,' Idris agrees, following us in. 'That was cringe-a-rella.'

'I thought I was quite brillendous,' I say, getting stuck into the washing up.

'You don't have to talk like that when you're with us,' Jess tuts. 'One Liam is more than enough. If you ask me I'd say you've done the dare and gone all crazy on the adrenalin.'

'Actually, I didn't do it. Zac just thinks I did.'

'You're joking?'

'Maddie wrote your name on the jar.

146

I was trying to take it out, when Fisher appeared from nowhere.'

'Yeah, about that,' Idris says, pulling out his phone.

IDRIS VOICEOVER: 'HERE IN THE WILDS OF AFRICA, WE FIND FRED DANGER ON ANOTHER INTREPID EXPEDITION.'

The camera pans round and Fred is squatting down next to the jars.

'I'M FRED DANGER,' he says. 'TO SURVIVE IN THE WILD YOU HAVE TO LIVE ON THE HEDGE. TODAY I BEEN PICKING UP BUGS WITH MY BARE HANDS. THIS IS A DEVIL'S COACH HORSE. WHICH ISN'T A COACH OR A HORSE. IT'S A BEETLE THAT SQUIRTS STINKY STUFF OUT OF ITS TUMMY. A BIT LIKE ME.'

COOL-O-METER

SUPERCOOL

CHILLING OUT

NO SWEAT

IN THE SHADE

COLD FEET

ON THIN ICE

LUKEWARM

HOT AND BOTHERED

SWEATING BUCKETS

TOTAL MELTDOWN

And he trumps, just as Billie Keegan
runs into shot and shouts: '*I CAN TRUMP
BETTERER!*' and she does, knocking
over the jars, and running off with Fred
chasing her.

Idris pans across and there's me dashing
towards the tent in an attempt to rescue
the jar, while Zac runs up to Mr Fisher
and points him in my direction. As Fisher
storms towards me, Zac and Maddie
high-five each other.

'I've cut the next scene. It's not pretty.'
'Appreciate that, Idris. But, oh my God,
he <u>WANTED</u> me to get caught!'
'They knew you'd try to take it back out,'
Idris says. 'The pair of them are criminal
masterminds. It's almost admirable . . .
except they're gits. We can't be sure what
game they're playing, but we need to be
playing it better.'
'It's like Scrabble!' Jess says. 'He puts
down a double-letter score, we need to put

down a triple-word score containing Q.'

Unfortunately I'm rubbish at Scrabble. Jess always tries to get me to play, but she knows all those annoying two-letter words that nobody's ever heard of. And all the five, six, and seven letter words too.

'Oi!' yells Mrs Fry, waving her whisk. 'This ain't no place for yakking! Shoo! I've already had stuff go walkabout!'

She herds us out of the kitchen. And I realize EXACTLY how to play our triple-word score.

In space no one can hear you scream. No one can hear you scream in a dormitory full of small-year-olds, either.

Sweeping the floor beneath Fred's bed has to go down as the WORST PUNISHMENT IN THE WORLD, because the woodlice are having a party with the snails and the damp socks and the indescribable thing that smells really bad.

COOL-O-METER

SUPERCOOL

CHILLING OUT

NO SWEAT

IN THE SHADE

COLD FEET

ON THIN ICE

LUKEWARM

HOT AND BOTHERED

SWEATING BUCKETS

TOTAL MELTDOWN

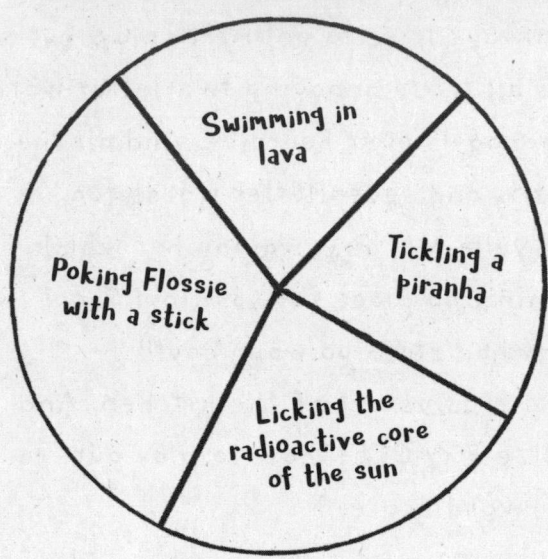

THINGS LESS HAZARDOUS THAN SWEEPING UNDER FRED'S BED

Swimming in lava

Tickling a piranha

Poking Flossie with a stick

Licking the radioactive core of the sun

'Leave Barbara alone!' Fred comes running in, spread-eagling on the duvet in an attempt to shield his woodlice.

'Don't worry, I'm not going anywhere near Barbara,' I say, heading to the girls' dorms. 'But you better take them back to the wood before Mrs Parker has a heart attack.'

All I want to do is finish sweeping, but another obstacle has presented itself: Flossie, who's stood next to her bed, which she's criss-crossed in sticky tape.

'My favourite unicorn water bottle's
gone missing, and this is a CRIME SCENE.
Don't fink I don't know what you're up to—
sweeping up the evidence!'

'Have you tried lost property?'

'I've already been fru the 'scusting box
that smells of teenagers.'

Billie Keegan comes stomping down the
dorm.

'I'm the bestest finderer. I'm great at
everyfing. Let me help.' She wipes her
fringe from her eyes.

'You need to go away,' Flossie shouts.
'I've got a lot on my plate. If Stan ain't
the thiever it's the deadly scarecrows, and
they'll be after my brains!'

'I'm sure there's a rational explanation,
Floss.'

'SNAIL RACE!' screams Fred, and the
whole lot of them rush to the end of the
dorm where he's set up a load of snails that
are sliming all over my newly swept floor.

COOL-O-METER

SUPERCOOL

CHILLING OUT

NO SWEAT

IN THE SHADE

COLD FEET

ON THIN ICE

LUKEWARM

HOT AND BOTHERED

SWEATING BUCKETS

TOTAL MELTDOWN

I watch Fred jump across the beds to get
to the finish line. Everything falls out of
his pockets—sticks, woodlice, more snails,
leaves and biscuits. He's never looked
happier, with no hint of homesickness.
He's certainly not missing the comfy chair
in the sunny spot by the window. Or Mum's
perfume when we come home from school.
Or Dad laughing at people falling over on
the telly while we eat beans on toast.

'COME ON, ANGUS! YOU CAN DO IT!'
he yells.

Dad always says missing things is a lot
like having a tooth filled. You feel horrible
pain at first, so it's best to take your mind
off it, because something will eventually
help fill the gap.

A snail race might not take my mind off
missing home, but I know what might.

I spot a bright white star moving quickly
from west to east. It can only be one thing.

'International Space Station!' I point.
'It's travelling about eight kilometres a
second. Has to go that fast or it would
crash to Earth.'

Already I'm feeling better as we lie in
the grass looking up at the early evening
sky, even if the clouds are creeping over.

'So it's like an ambush?' Jess studies my
hastily drawn-up chart with a torch.

'Run it past me one more time,' Idris says.

'Sorry guys, I'd have done a full pres-
entation if I'd had time. The main thing is,
don't fall asleep.'

'And you're sure this is going to work?'

'Relax Jess, it'll be fine,' I say, putting
my hands behind my head. 'There's nothing
like staring into space to help calm you
down. It really brings home the fact you're
pinned down by gravity to a rock with
active tectonic plates that's spinning about
1,600 kilometres an hour in the never-ending nothingness of space.'

'That's supposed to help?' Jess sits up.

COOL-O-METER

SUPERCOOL

CHILLING OUT

NO SWEAT

IN THE SHADE

COLD FEET

ON THIN ICE

LUKEWARM

HOT AND BOTHERED

SWEATING BUCKETS

TOTAL MELTDOWN

'Yeah, that's not really working for me, either,' Idris agrees.

'We need to focus. Tonight is my initiation. Finally I'll learn ALL their secrets. Maybe why they wear sunglasses indoors. And when all goes to plan,' I sit up half-smirking, 'I can Stanipulate the situation and we'll finally get revenge.'

'Did you just say Stanipulate?' Jess shines the torch in my face.

'All right, don't have a Stantrum.'

'Seriously, Stan, you have to stop.' Idris helps me to my feet. 'You're way too chirpy for someone about to go through an initiation. You do know what it involves?'

I don't have a clue, thanks to The Dog rules of never talking about The Dogs. And knowing Zac, it isn't going to be pretty.

⤷ INITIATION

**STANLEY WINSTON FOX'S
LAST WILL AND TESTAMENT**

In the event of a calamity befalling me during the initiation to THE DOGS (which is quite likely, let's be honest), I bequeath the following possessions:

☆ Pocket money, meteorite, and manners – FRED

☆ My younger brother – LIAM

☆ Lego Death Star (may need rebuilding, because: Fred), and a stack of fun word searches – IDRIS

☆ Telescope – GRAN

☆ Any of Gran's leftover cake – MUM (so she can finally see what cake should taste like)

☆ How to BBQ Successfully book – DAD

☆ Diagram notebooks – JESS, so she can sell my memoirs which will be talked about for centuries, and maybe a newly discovered star will be named after me as a mark of respect.

COOL-O-METER

SUPERCOOL
CHILLING OUT
NO SWEAT
IN THE SHADE
COLD FEET
THIN ON ICE
LUKEWARM
HOT AND BOTHERED
SWEATING BUCKETS
TOTAL MELTDOWN

I knock on the door, quickly stuffing my socks in my pockets now that bare ankles are back in again. Mason opens it, and grabs me by the collar.

'Mostly c,' he whispers. 'He's mostly c, isn't he?'

'Eh?'

But Zac interrupts.

'What's the delay, M-Dog? Let him in.'

I walk into almost darkness. The curtains are pulled, and everyone's stood in a circle shining torches on their faces, which are painted with stripy patterns.

Zac points to the chair in the centre.

'L-Dog, inform him of our motto.'

'DARES ARE THE GAME—PASS THE BLAME, DODGE THE SHAME,' Liam recites, as Zac takes out a tube of toothpaste.

'The African wild dog is also known as the painted wolf. No two dogs have the same markings.'

He squirts toothpaste stripes across my eyebrows and above my top lip.

156

'We are The Dogs,' everyone chants. 'A-WOOOOOO!'

Liam nudges me to howl along with them, as Zac takes off one of his many leather bracelets and fastens it around my wrist.

'This is the AMULET OF DECEPTION. It represents an unbroken circle of getting away with stuff. By wearing it, you stay faithful to our cause.'

He takes out a pair of sunglasses and places them on my face.

'These are the SUNGLASSES OF CONCEALMENT. Wear them indoors and nobody can see the guilt in your eyes. Now you're ready—'

'Oh! That wasn't so bad!'

'—for the initiation,' Zac announces. 'The Dog Dare.'

Pants. Knew it was too easy.

'Does he HAVE to do it?' Liam asks.

'All of us had to do it, L-Dog.'

Tash walks over with two slices of bread and gently pats my shoulder, as Zac opens

COOL-O-METER

SUPERCOOL

CHILLING OUT

NO SWEAT

IN THE SHADE

COLD FEET

ON THIN ICE

LUKEWARM

HOT AND BOTHERED

SWEATING BUCKETS

TOTAL MELTDOWN

his rucksack and takes out a can of dog
food.

'Gulp. Can I pee up against a lamp post
instead? Or lick someone's face?'

'It's a dog-food sandwich. End of.'

I'd happily trade that for Mum's beetroot
cake. Even the parsnip muffins. Maybe not
pea brownies though.

'Unless . . .' Zac stops talking so his
brain can think. 'You tell us Alaska's other
names.'

I grab it. *STEAK AND KIDNEY PIE,
STEAK AND KIDNEY PIE,* I keep telling
myself, as I take a bite, quickly chewing and
swallowing, washing it down with water.

'Welcome to The Dogs!' Zac slaps me on
the back and I almost throw up.

'A-WOOOOOOOOOO!' they all howl.

'Now it's time for a scary film!' Zac grins.

'Um, I could really do with some literally
artisan food after that.' I put my hand up.
'Y'know, like that buffet we had the other day.'

'Why not,' Zac agrees. 'Will only take five

minutes to grab stuff from the kitchens.'

'And I can fetch some tasty cake,' I say, knowing full well I can't because it contains peas.

'Decent. Meet back here.'

'Idris! Wake up!' I whisper, shaking him.

'Elbow lasers or harpoon eyes?' he mumbles in his sleep.

'Idris!'

'Eh? Oh, it's you. What you wearing sunglasses for?'

'I'm officially a Dog. The plan is on. I've woken Jess; she's doing her bit, come on!'

He puts on his dressing gown and slippers. We tiptoe through the corridor, open the door and creep outside. A sliver of moonlight illuminates the camp in shades of grey, and I could seriously do with the elephant hawk moth's ability to see colour at night.

'There he is!' Idris says in my ear.

COOL-O-METER

SUPERCOOL

CHILLING OUT

NO SWEAT

IN THE SHADE

COLD FEET

ON THIN ICE

LUKEWARM

HOT AND BOTHERED

SWEATING BUCKETS

TOTAL MELTDOWN

We watch a figure tiptoe through the toadstools to The Downtime Hut, then walk straight into some wind chimes. They quickly disappear round the side of the building towards the kitchen window.

'We have to wake Fisher,' I say, and start heading to his tent.

The adrenaline kicks in and I feel a bit sick, especially as he's snoring loudly. It's like waking a bear who hasn't been able to hibernate for weeks, but has finally fallen asleep, and definitely won't want waking up.

As soon as we get close, Idris shoves me forward.

'No way I'm doing it.'

I knock on the fabric. Obviously it makes no sound at all.

'What are you knocking for?' he hisses. 'It's a tent!'

'I know!' I hiss back. 'But I'm scared.'

'Make an owl noise or something.'

'TAWIT-A-TAWOO!' I whisper-shout.

'Seriously?' Idris stares at me. 'Have you

ever heard an owl make
that noise? It sounds like
you're *IN PAIN*.'

'What, so you're an owl expert all
of a sudden?'

'For a start, it's more like a HE-HICK,
followed by a HOOO-OOO-OOO-OOO, and
one owl is calling the other owl. It's not all
coming from the same one. Vary it a bit.'

'All right, David Attenborough, why don't
you do it? But get a move—'

'WHAT *ON EARTH IS GOING ON*?'
Mr Fisher's head yells, poking out of
the tent and peering up at us.

'Gulp. Sorry, Sir.'

'Why are you out of bed?'

We look at each other.

'Sir, quick, there's a thief in the
kitchens!' Idris points.

I can't believe Mr Fisher has camouflage
pyjamas, I think to myself as we hurry
through the camp. Then we all stop in our
tracks as we spot a torchlight flashing

COOL-O-METER

SUPERCOOL
CHILLING OUT
NO SWEAT
IN THE SHADE
COLD FEET
ON THIN ICE
LUKEWARM
HOT AND BOTHERED
SWEATING BUCKETS
TOTAL MELTDOWN

around inside.

'My goodness, there is a thief! Um, maybe we should wake another teacher . . .'

'Everyone stay back!' Petra calls, running across camp followed by Jess. 'Norman and I will deal with this.'

'We will?' Mr Fisher squeaks, as Petra takes out a key and unlocks the Downtime Hut. She walks purposefully over to the kitchen, as we sneak in and hide behind a table. My heart's thumping—finally Zac's going to get his comeuppance.

Petra flicks on a light-switch, and yells: 'Put your hands up and step away from the fridge!'

As the figure turns around, Mr Fisher lets out a scream—it's a zombie. Not an actual zombie, but Zac Cassidy in his zombie mask, who freezes in terror at being caught and drops an armful of baguettes.

'Who've we got here?' Petra moves forward and pulls off the mask as we strain to see the look on his face.

'Liam Miller!' Mr Fisher bellows, turning

Hot Lava Red. 'What on earth do you think you're doing?'

'LIAM?' we all whisper, and duck behind the table again.

'Sorry,' he shuffles his feet. 'I've got . . . baguette deficiency. Need at least four a day.'

'What you need is to be up at six to help Mrs Fry serve breakfast. And lunch. And dinner. It might make up for eating half her larder.' Mr Fisher shakes his head. 'Let's all get back to bed before that infernal cockerel starts cock-a-doodle-do-ing.'

As Petra locks the kitchen window, we quickly scramble back to the Slumber Shack before Liam spots us.

'Well, that back-fired,' Idris says, as we sneak through the corridor. The light's off in Zac and Mason's room, with no hint of a scary film, so we clamber into bed.

'Everything all right, mate-bro?' I whisper, as Liam wanders in.

'I got caught,' he scratches his head. 'Bad

COOL-O-METER

SUPERCOOL

CHILLING OUT

NO SWEAT

IN THE SHADE

COLD FEET

ON THIN ICE

LUKEWARM

HOT AND BOTHERED

SWEATING BUCKETS

TOTAL MELTDOWN

luckington or what?'

'That's REALLY bad luckington,' I say, feeling guilty. But I'm convinced luckington had nothing to do with it. Zac knew what we were up to, and I've finally worked out the real game he's playing, because he's trumped me in every category.

WHO'S THE BEST?

ZAC

Brilliant trainers 11
Cool hair 100
Effortless style.............. Obvs
Getting away with it... Expert

WHO'S THE BEST?

STAN

Brilliant trainers 0
Cool hair .... -20
Effortless style.............. Nope
Getting away with it.....Never

⤷ SHORTCUT OF DOOM

Every living thing on Earth evolved from a bacterium that lived billions of years ago. Some things have clearly advanced more than others, and I feel I need to get smarter.

'Stan,' Idris says over breakfast. 'I think we're going to need a bigger chart.'

Not even wholemeal pancakes can fill the guilty hole I'm feeling in the pit of my stomach, especially as Liam has to help serve them up.

'Why does Zac get away with it every single time?'

'Because he's playing Battleships—it's a game of strategy, and he keeps sinking our chances of winning. And I do not like losing. Especially sleep,' Jess yawns.

SUPERCOOL

CHILLING OUT

NO SWEAT

IN THE SHADE

COLD FEET

ON THIN ICE

COOL-O-METER

LUKEWARM

HOT AND BOTHERED

SWEATING BUCKETS

TOTAL MELTDOWN

Maddie spots her and walks over with Zac.

'I guess you don't get much sleep in the land of the midnight sun.'

'Well done on finding out another fact about Alaska. Want a medal?' Jess tuts.

'Hey, we've bigger things to think about,' Zac says. 'I feel immensely bad about L-Dog getting caught.'

He sits down next to us and has no trouble scoffing four pancakes.

'L-Dog volunteered cos he wanted to get you something decent from the kitchens, but Fisher must have heard him.'

'Yeah,' I glance at Idris, feeling guiltier. 'He must have.'

'No more kitchen supplies for us.' He shrugs. 'Guess I'm going to have to come up with another super-dare. Oh, I have, and you're going to love it. It's the perfect way to make it up to Liam and get ourselves a fresh supply of snacks.'

'How?' I ask.

'Not here. Meet up Scrambly Hill—we've

been given free time this afternoon. Which is just enough time for a trip to the sweet shop.'

'This is more like it!' Mr Fisher says, doing some back stretches. 'An old-fashioned obstacle course.'

'Ah, but we've 360-degreed-it, Norm.' Rufus slaps him on the back. 'Everyone's going to do it tied together in groups—it's time for half-past team-building!'

I actually hear Mr Fisher sigh.

'Yes it IS exciting. Here's your chance to balance like agile squirrels, climb like mountain goats, and swing like capuchin monkeys! The course will take you right around the wood and once you get to the end there's some level-up amazement—a zip wire!'

Which is amazing to everyone but me because I'm scared of heights.

'Finally,' Jess punches the air. 'A slight element of danger with a strong harness.'

Even Fred karate chops the air—Flint

COOL-O-METER

SUPERCOOL

CHILLING OUT

NO SWEAT

IN THE SHADE

COLD FEET

THIN ON THIN ICE

LUKEWARM

HOT AND BOTHERED

SWEATING BUCKETS

TOTAL MELTDOWN

Danger frequently travels by zip wire.

'Liam Miller!' Mr Fisher yells. 'Do you *ever* stop eating? Give me ten squat jumps—'

Petra interrupts and asks Liam if he'd like to offer up ten signs of spring instead. I can almost hear his brain clunking.

'Um . . . nine Easter eggs in the shops . . . and bluebells?'

'Maybe feature some wildlife in your lesson plan, Norm?' Petra winks. 'Start with the Common Froghopper, a bug that can leap seventy centimetres in the air.'

She points to a stinging nettle covered in what looks like spit.

'This is a Froghopper baby—a larvae that sucks the sap from plants. It protects itself in a frothy mass of bubbles which it squeezes from its bottom.'

'I wish I could do that,' Fred says dreamily.

'Water those thoughts, little fella. Who knows what you could do.' Rufus ruffles his hair. 'Get into your teams, dudes, and let's three-hundred-per-cent it!'

Imagine how much fun doing an obstacle course would be if you were tied to your mates. And then un-imagine that because you get teamed with Zac and Mason.

FIVE PLACES I'D RATHER BE THAN TIED TO ZAC AND MASON

1. Mr Fisher's algebra lesson in a fug-filled classroom when everyone's eaten Mrs Gravy's bean hotpot.
2. Under Fred's dormitory bed with his woodlice village.
3. In assembly singing SEARCH FOR THE HERO in front of the whole school.
4. On a zip wire.
5. At a tarantula barbecue.

'I know a shortcut,' Zac says, linking the rope to the clips around our waists. 'It'll miss out most of the lame obstacles and get us on the zip wire first. Then we'll have loads of free time.'

COOL-O-METER

SUPERCOOL

CHILLING OUT

NO SWEAT

IN THE SHADE

COLD FEET

ON THIN ICE

LUKEWARM

HOT AND BOTHERED

SWEATING BUCKETS

TOTAL MELTDOWN

'Oh. I was looking forward to the scramble net,' Mason says, using actual words.

'And what about our mentor duties?' I say as Zac starts to drag us away.

'There's more parent helpers than kids; we won't be missed. And I get away with stuff like this all the time.'

I don't have much choice, seeing as I'm attached to him. When no one's looking, he leads us through a patch of stinging nettles, with no regard for bare ankles.

'Um, we're not on the path,' I point out, as we pass the hollowed oak tree.

'Who cares, keep up.'

It's hard to with Mason's large stride, as they lead me into a dense patch of wood where we have to fight our way through brambles, climb over a fallen tree, and leap ditches. It would have been easier to do the course.

'How DO you get away with stuff all the time?' I ask.

'I outsmart everyone because of my literally brilliant brain.' He turns up his collar. 'And

I surround myself with people who will do anything for me. While you're writing swotty diaries in the Downtime Hut, Mason does mine. Leaves me more time for gaming in my room.'

He leads us under a prickly holly bush and out towards a hut among the trees.

'Time for refreshments,' he says, opening the door and pulling us inside. 'They keep loads of stuff in here—including food.'

He gets Mason to shift crates so we can sit down, then grabs a pack of biscuits and a flask.

'Saw the parent helpers in here the other day—they're allowed to use it for tea breaks.'

'What is all this?' I rummage through the crates, some of which are filled with gold-painted pine cones. 'Christmas decorations?'

'Might be useful. Especially on the last day.'

'How do you know?'

'Benefits of being a teacher's pet—but I wouldn't want to spoil the surprise. Second thoughts, maybe if you spilled Alaska's full

SUPERCOOL

CHILLING OUT

NO SWEAT

IN THE SHADE

COLD FEET

ON THIN ICE

COOL-O-METER

LUKEWARM

HOT AND BOTHERED

SWEATING BUCKETS

TOTAL MELTDOWN

name.'

'I've told you before, I don't know anything. And her name's Jess.'

'I bet you've got a diagram all about it. That's what you do, isn't it? Chart Geek.'

'How do you decide which chart to do?' Mason uses actual words again.

'Well sometimes it's obvious, y'know, the best way to present the information. But other times it takes careful consider—'

'You're not s'pose to be encouraging him!' Zac chucks a pine cone at Mason's head. 'And where's your yo-yo?'

'Um, I thought I wouldn't carry a menacing prop from now on.'

'I don't believe what I'm hearing. You're my henchman, M-Dog; it's what you do.'

'Right, yeah, sorry,' he says, taking it out and spinning it.

'The other thing we do is TRESPASS.'

He drags us back outside, down into a ditch and up to a fence with a big sign saying KEEP OUT. And for good reason.

It's the farmer's boggy field. And there in the middle is a scarecrow, staring ominously at me with his button eyes.

'This is the edge of camp. We shouldn't go beyond this, really.' I try to act nonchalant. 'I mean, it doesn't bother me, it's just—'

'It's the shortcut, numpty.' Zac climbs through it. 'We cut across this field, back through the fence on the other side, and the zip wire's right there.'

Mason is already through and pulling me by the rope.

'Um, I might sit this one out guys, y'know, after tentgate.' I unclip it and go to turn back.

'Liam will think you're cool if you do this,' Zac shouts after me. 'You never do anything fun; that's why he started hanging out with me.'

'That's not true. I always do fun stuff with Liam. Only last week I drew up a bar chart analysing the fun stuff we'd done in February. Including playing chess with crisps.'

COOL-O-METER

SUPERCOOL

CHILLING OUT

NO SWEAT

IN THE SHADE

COLD FEET

ON THIN ICE

LUKEWARM

HOT AND BOTHERED

SWEATING BUCKETS

TOTAL MELTDOWN

TURN SIDEWAYS FOR
MY AMAZING GRAPH

STAN AND LIAM'S BAR CHART OF FUN (FEBRUARY)

So fun I forgot
I was trying to
have fun

Actual proper
fun

Only I thought
it was fun

Fair to
middling
fun

Not fun

Regrettable

Playing chess
with crisps

Talking
backwards for
a whole day

Sorting my
planet books in
order of mass

Adding chocolate
to a pizza

Seeing who could
stay awake all night
at Idris's sleepover

'What crisp was the knight?' Mason asks.

'A Monster Munch.'

'Nice.'

Zac stares at us both again.

'You two seriously need to shut up about charts. C'mon!'

I look behind me and realize I don't know my way back, having forgotten Gran's advice about leaving a trail of wool behind me. Then Liam's voice echoes in my head again 'YOU'RE JUST A BIT . . . NOT SPONTANEOUS SOMETIMES, STAN.' Maybe my BAR CHART OF FUN needs shaking up a bit. Maybe it's time to hit the cool bell again.

I climb through, and don't take my eyes off the scarecrow, which is why it takes four footsteps before I'm completely stuck. And I'm not the only one.

'I can't move!' Mason grunts, as the rope goes taut and Zac almost falls backwards. Luckily I'm not still tied to them as they have a mini tug-of-war.

COOL-O-METER

SUPERCOOL

CHILLING OUT

NO SWEAT

IN THE SHADE

COLD FEET

THIN ICE

LUKEWARM

HOT AND BOTHERED

SWEATING BUCKETS

TOTAL MELTDOWN

'That's called inappropriate footwear.
If you had Earth Whisperers like me you
wouldn't get stuck.'

He pulls the rope and Mason falls onto
his hands.

'It stinks!' he moans.

The breeze picks up and the scarecrow's
raggedy clothes start flapping in the wind.

'Wait! What's that?' Mason whispers,
using his deer ears.

At first it sounds like a woodpecker and
I can't tell where it's coming from. Then
a haunting, creaking noise reverberates
around us.

'Oh my God!' he shrieks. 'It's the scarecrow
coming to life! Let's get out of here!'

I try to prize my foot from the mud.

'The scarecrow's going to eat your
brains!' Zac laughs, tugging the rope so
Mason is dragged free, but they can't
pull me out because I unclipped it.

'Help!'

'Tell me Alaska's whole name, and I might.'

I hear another noise. A grunting, beastly noise. The sort of noise that makes you pull the duvet up round your ears after watching a scary film.

'Let's get out of here!' Mason squeals, reaching across with a dead branch and dragging me free.

'Leg it!' Zac shouts, and we all run in the opposite direction, away from the bog, and under the fence.

My heart's pounding, but I don't look back. Before I know it, we're out through a hedge and onto the course by the scramble net that leads to the zip wire.

'I'm never going back there!' Mason clutches his side, as Zac starts laughing.

'That was crazy.' And I laugh too.

The adrenalin makes me forget my fear of heights as I climb to the top ready to be attached to the zip wire. I feel I can do anything. This must be what Liam meant about being in The Dogs—the thrill of getting away with it. It makes up for all the times

SUPERCOOL
CHILLING OUT
NO SWEAT
IN THE SHADE
COLD FEET
THIN ICE
COOL-O-METER
LUKEWARM
HOT AND BOTHERED
SWEATING BUCKETS
TOTAL MELTDOWN

you've been caught.

I launch off the top, scared for a split second, then laugh in the wind as I zoom down the wire, not caring about heights at all.

I draw closer and closer to Mr Fisher who's waiting for me as I crash into the net. Oh God. He knows I've just broken rule number twenty-five. It's all over.

'Well, well, Mr Fox.' He unclips me. 'I didn't think you had it in you.'

'Um, Sir, I, er—'

'You've overcome your fear of heights,' he smiles.

'Oh . . . yes, I suppose I have,' I say, pretty sure guilt is written all over my face. I quickly put on my Sunglasses of Concealment and Zac high-fives me.

I feel . . . amazesome.

'A-WOOOOOOOOO!' I howl.

↳ WALKING TALLER

I feel giddy, like I'm floating in space. Although floating in actual space can be a tiring experience—it's difficult to move in a spacesuit, and to top it all you're wearing a nappy.

Not only did I conquer my fear of heights, but for once I was spontaneous and fun.

And part of me wants to do it again.

THE BATTLE OF MY INNER MES RIGHT NOW

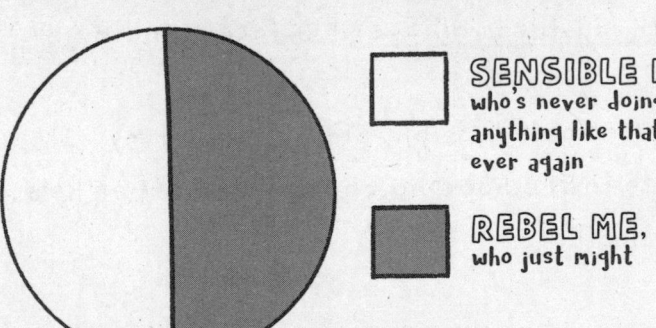

SENSIBLE ME, who's never doing anything like that ever again

REBEL ME, who just might

COOL-O-METER

SUPERCOOL
CHILLING OUT
NO SWEAT
IN THE SHADE
COLD FEET
ON THIN ICE
LUKEWARM
HOT AND BOTHERED
SWEATING BUCKETS
TOTAL MELTDOWN

'It's hard to explain,' I say, as we eat carrot and hummus wraps on the grass. 'But when you do a dare and actually get away with it, it's amazesome. And there's no denying Zac IS cool, even if the shortcut was WELL creepy. No way I'm ever going back there.'

'You've gone to the dark side too, mate,' Idris tuts.

'I just see things a bit differently now,' I say, adjusting my sunglasses. 'But I can't say any more because the first rule of The Dogs is—'

'You're all idiots.' Jess shakes her head. 'You'd be feeling differently right now if you'd got caught—and he'd blame it all on you.'

Suddenly everyone starts screaming as Fred comes running through the picnic area with ladybirds all over his face, sending fruit flying.

'Not again,' I sigh, hiding behind my plate in the hope no one will remember he's my brother.

'*AGAIN?*' Idris says filming him.

'He's trying to copy Flint Danger's bee beard—episode twelve, when he's still trying to prove his manliness.'

At least it's not as bad as last time, when he ran through the house while Mum was entertaining the neighbours with a cold meat buffet.

'Woah, little fella!' Rufus grabs him, and spins him around so the ladybirds fly off. 'See this stinky yellow liquid? That's ladybird blood. They leak it from their knees when you scare them. Leave them on the plants, dude, not on your face.'

'I didn't mean to hurt them.' Fred frowns as Rufus takes him to the stream to wash it off. 'Does Angus bleed from his knees?'

'No, but I'm sure he'd rather be totally in the fresh air than in your pocket, no matter how much you love him.'

Fred takes Angus out and holds him in his palm.

'Can Angus have another snail fact?'

181

CHILLING OUT

NO SWEAT

IN THE SHADE

COLD FEET

COOL-O-METER

THIN ON ICE

LUKEWARM

HOT AND BOTHERED

SWEATING BUCKETS

TOTAL MELTDOWN

'Of course. How about his cousin that lives at the bottom of the ocean where the seawater is heated by molten lava. The scaly-foot snail has evolved a shell of interlocking iron-based plates.' Rufus leans in. 'It's like he's wearing a SUIT OF ARMOUR.'

'Snails are brilliant!' Fred has to sit down he's so amazed. 'I wish Angus had a suit of armour to stop fings haxidentally stamping on him.'

'Is that why you carry him everywhere? Cos unless he's outside, Fred, he won't grow a healthy shell. You think you're protecting him, but you're probably not, dude.'

'PLATES! GIMME YOUR PLATES!' Liam interrupts, collecting stuff to take to the kitchen in his never-ending punishment for trying to steal baguettes. 'I'm living an actual daymare. I've never chopped so many organic vegetables.'

'Sorry mate,' I wince, as a feeling of guilt makes my insides churn.

'It's not your fault. Better go, I've got to

throw together a cauliflower casserole with quinoa. And the tragedy is, I know what that means,' he moans, starting to wander back. 'Enjoy your free time, guy-bros.'

Mr Fisher's been called back to school for a meeting and we've been relieved of mentor duties—what should be a brilliant afternoon is now rubbish because my best mate is shut up in a kitchen. And all because of me.

'Why don't we meet Zac up Scrambly Hill?' I shrug. 'See what this sweet shop idea is? He's not all bad, y'know.'

'You should see this,' says Idris. 'While you were out in No Stan's Land, I filmed Fred.'

He takes out his phone.

IDRIS VOICEOVER: 'HERE IN PAPUA NEW GUINEA, WE FIND INTREPID EXPLORER FRED DANGER.'

The camera pans round and zooms in on Fred who is hiding in a bush.

COOL-O-METER

SUPERCOOL

CHILLING OUT

NO SWEAT

IN THE SHADE

COLD FEET

THIN ON ICE

LUKEWARM

HOT AND BOTHERED

SWEATING BUCKETS

TOTAL MELTDOWN

'I'M FRED DANGER,' he says. 'TO SURVIVE IN THE WILD YOU HAVE TO LIVE ON THE HEDGE. TODAY I'M BEING A FROGHOPPER AND SQUEEZING BUBBLES OUT OF MY—'

'CUT!' Idris yells. 'SORRY FRED, BUT NOBODY NEEDS TO SEE THAT.'

He zooms in on Jess whizzing down the zip wire.

'CAN I DO IT AGAIN?' she says, wiping her brow.

'WATCH YOU DON'T GET TOO HOT, OR YOU'LL BE BAKED, ALASKA!' Maddie shouts after her.

Then I come zooming down with a massive grin on my face, as Zac high-fives me at the bottom. Idris pans the camera and zooms in on Mason and Tash.

'IT WASN'T JUST A SHORTCUT, HE'S

ON A RECONNAISSANCE MISSION FOR
THE SUPER-DARE. I'M WORRIED ABOUT
IT, TASH. THERE'S SOMETHING DODGY
ABOUT THAT PLACE.'

'Y'KNOW WHAT, MASON?' Tash says.
'I'M NOT FINDING THE DOGS THAT FUN
ANY MORE. I'M FED UP WITH ALWAYS
BEING ZAC'S LOOK-OUT. I NEED TO
START LOOKING OUT FOR MYSELF,
METAPHORICALLY AS WELL AS LOOKING
WHERE I'M GOING. I'M THINKING OF,
LIKE, QUITTING.'

'ME TOO. BUT YOU KNOW HE WON'T
LET US. BECAUSE OF—'

'SSSH, HE'S COMING.'

'The Dogs are starting to fall apart!'
Jess grins. 'Suddenly it's a game of Happy
Families, and pretty soon we'll be holding
all the cards.'

'D'you think you've been spending too
much time in the Board Games Gazebo?'

'As if you could ever do that, Stan!' she

COOL-O-METER

SUPERCOOL

CHILLING OUT

NO SWEAT

IN THE SHADE

COLD FEET

ON THIN ICE

LUKEWARM

HOT AND BOTHERED

SWEATING BUCKETS

TOTAL MELTDOWN

says jumping up. 'C'mon! We've got an appointment up Scrambly Hill.'

'All you've got to do is jump the ditch, walk down the field and cross the camp boundary.' Zac points into the distance, towards a fence. 'It's only one more field after that; you'll be there and back in no time. And with Fisher gone it's not even a dare—just a nice stroll with mates.'

'You're absolutely sure it's a sweet shop?' Idris squints. 'And it's only a COUPLE of fields.'

'Of course. We saw it through the telescope didn't we, S-Dog?'

'It's true. There's a big sweet sign.'

'I'd go myself but Rufus has got me teaching bird species to the small-year-olds. Yawn united. Anyway, I got you these.' He takes something out of a carrier bag.

It's a pair of designer trainers so dazzlingly bright that the sun reflects off them and almost blinds me.

'You can have them. You NEED them.'
He turns his nose up at my bog-soaked
canvas pumps.

They fit perfectly. I turn my foot to see
the logos glinting.

'I don't know what to say . . . thanks.'

'S'cool. And you can have this, Idris.' He
hands over his wallet. 'Buy all the sweets
you want, stock up the jacket cupboard.'

'Oh . . .' Idris thumbs through it. 'That'll
buy LOADS of sweets.'

'Yep. And this is for you, Alask—, I mean,
Jess. It's an electronic book. You can get,
like, a billion books on it or sommat. I've
never used it.'

'Um . . . OK.' She takes it. 'We'll do it
on one condition. You make Stan your second-in-command.'

'Wow. I mean, if you do this, you'll be
heroes for bringing back treats. Why not?'

I guess it would be the perfect way to
make it up to Liam. I could explain about

SUPERCOOL
CHILLING OUT
NO SWEAT
IN THE SHADE
COLD FEET
ON THIN ICE
LUKEWARM
HOT AND BOTHERED
SWEATING BUCKETS
TOTAL MELTDOWN

COOL-O-METER

the kitchen ambush while he had a mouthful
of sweets so he couldn't shout at me.
Plus I'm hoping for that joyful feeling of
getting away with something again. I pop
on my sunglasses.

'A-WOOOOOOOOO!'

'Is the howling thing really necessary?'
Jess asks, as I duck under some wire and
jump the ditch.

'It's what we do in The Dogs,' I say,
starting to head down the field. 'But I can't
tell you any more because—'

'Why are we trusting him again?' Idris
says, trying to catch me up.

'Um, hello! He gave us stuff!' I say with
a spring in my step because the trainers
make me feel taller. 'I mean, there's loads of
money in that wallet! And you must be happy
Jess, thousands of books in one hand?'

'That isn't the reason I'm doing this!' She
leaps over the ditch and stops us in our

tracks. 'It's not even like I can smell the pages. Sometimes I worry about you, Stan. You really think there's a sweet shop two fields away?'

'Er—'

'Because there isn't. It's a garage called SWEET WHEELS. And it's at least *FIVE* fields away including one full of cows and cow pats. Thank God <u>ONE</u> of us was paying attention on the coach ride in.'

'Are you sure?'

'Would you rather believe Jess, who's been your mate since you were five?' Idris asks. 'Or Mr Lied-About-Everything-Since-We-Got-Here?'

'Um . . .'

'The minute we go over the camp boundary, what do you think he's going to do, Stan?' She points to the fence up ahead with a large Keep Out sign.

KEEP OUT

SUPERCOO
CHILLING OUT
NO SWEAT
IN THE SHADE
COLD FEET
ON THIN ICE
LUKEWARM
HOT AND BOTHERED
SWEATING BUCKETS
TOTAL MELTDOWN
COOL-O-METER

'Run and tell Rufus,' I whisper, removing the Sunglasses of Concealment. It's like they've got some sort of magical power which fuzzes my mind and turns me into an idiot. 'Can't believe I've been oblivious. I should have Stanticipated this.'

'You should have left that word in your brain,' Jess tuts. 'The last thing Zac's expecting us to do is stay on camp and still return with sweets, but that's exactly what we ARE going to do.'

'How?'

'Follow me!'

She leads us back across the ditch, through some trees behind The Downtime Hut, and down a path towards a porta cabin with a sign saying 'The Touch Base'.

'Get down!' she orders, making us duck under the windows. 'Just got to check no one's inside.'

'What is this place?'

'The staff room,' she says, trying the door, but it's locked. 'It's where all the teachers touch base.'

'Wow. That just made me feel a bit nauseous.' Idris pulls a face. 'They'll be having idea showers next.'

Jess pulls at an open window and unhooks the latch.

'Um, we're not going to nick stuff are we?'

'What do you take me for, Stan?' she says. 'It will all be perfectly legal and above board. Apart from maybe this bit.'

With a leg-up from Idris, she climbs inside.

'You sure about this?' I gulp, as I help Idris through the window.

Before I know it, they've pulled me inside too. We're standing in a room with comfy chairs, filing cabinets, Rufus's ukulele, and a coffee pot percolating on a table. And there in the corner is a small vending machine.

'Rufus and Petra act like they only eat organic chickpeas, but when we're not looking they're chomping on chocolate bars,' Jess whispers. 'Caught them at it

COOL-O-METER

SUPERCOOL
CHILLING OUT
NO SWEAT
IN THE SHADE
COLD FEET
THIN ICE
LUKEWARM
HOT AND BOTHERED
SWEATING BUCKETS
TOTAL MELTDOWN

when I had to hand in the catapult.'

'This is genius, Jess!' Idris starts feeding money into the machine and punching codes.

'We'll have to be quick.' I chew my lip. 'They could be back any minute for their coffee.'

The coils start to rotate slowly and, one by one, the treats drop to the bottom, which Jess grabs and shoves in her rucksack. I pace up and down by the window, looking for any sign of adults, while adrenalin plays leapfrog with my heart.

'Hurry it up, guys!'

'Just one more . . .' Idris says. 'There's a Kit Kat in here!'

'C'mon! I can hear someone coming!'

Idris takes the rest of the money from Zac's wallet and stuffs it into a SAVE THE TREES charity box. We quickly fumble back through the window as Jess replaces the latch, then hide at the back of the porta cabin, just as Rufus appears, humming and unlocking the door to The Touch Base.

There's a sound of jangling coins, the whirr of the vending machine, and then silence. Jess slowly peers through the window.

'It's OK,' she whispers. 'He's eating a Kit Kat.'

'That was MY Kit Kat!' Idris hisses.

'Can we just get out of here?' I gesture madly.

We sneak into the trees and head back to camp where everyone's chilling in hammocks and playing board games. The Dogs are flicking sticks at whoever walks under the reading tree. Which right now is us.

'Back early?' Zac jumps down. 'Knew you'd chicken out. Shame. Thought you actually had it in you to do something cool.'

Jess empties the rucksack and the treats fall to the ground at his feet. His mouth drops open.

'Woah! You guys DID do something cool.' Tash fist-bumps us. 'Respect!'

'That is a PROPER haul,' Mason grins.

'What's all this!' Liam shows up, having

SUPERCOOL
CHILLING OUT
NO SWEAT
IN THE SHADE
COLD FEET
THIN ON ICE
LUKEWARM
HOT AND BOTHERED
SWEATING BUCKETS
TOTAL MELTDOWN

COOL-O-METER

finally been freed from his kitchen im-
prisonment.

'For you, mate-bro,' I say, handing him
three chocolate bars.

'Brillendous!'

'All right, calm down, it's not THAT
brillendous,' Zac sneers.

'So I guess this makes Stan your second-in-command now?' Jess says. 'And a
big say in what you do?'

'Hey!' Maddie shouts, having ignored us
up until now. 'That's my job!'

'Mads, it's fine, I got this. Think it's
time for a meeting.'

He leads me, Jess and Idris up to the
Slumber Shack, through the patio doors and
into his room.

'Congratulations.' He starts slow clapping
us. 'You outsmarted me. Or at least you
think you did. You forgot I've got a literally
brilliant brain.'

'What's wrong, Zac? Worried you're
starting to lose that tight leash you've got

on The Dogs?' Jess says.

'Where'd you get all the sweets from? And where's my wallet?' he snarls, as Idris throws it at him. 'You seriously spent ALL of it?'

'Because we weren't supposed to spend any, were we?' I say. 'You knew it wasn't a sweet shop!'

'Whatever. Anyway, I'm officially making you a stray—you're no longer in The Dogs. As if you'd be my second-in-command. Trying to trick me is totally NOT cool. Oh. And neither is trying to film me.'

'Dunno what you're talking about.' Idris tries to shrug nonchalantly.

'Yes, you do. I've seen you with your phone—spying on conversations and trying to catch me out.'

'I'm making a David Attenborough documentary—you just happened to get in the way.'

'I know EXACTLY what you've been up to. But guess what? You're not the only one

SUPERCOOL

CHILLING OUT

NO SWEAT

IN THE SHADE

COLD FEET

ON THIN ICE

COOL-O-METER

LUKEWARM

HOT AND BOTHERED

SWEATING BUCKETS

TOTAL MELTDOWN

who brought a phone. And you're not the only one who's been making a documentary.'

He takes out a mobile and plays a clip of us jumping the ditch.

'So?' Idris shrugs.

'Oh, did I not tell you?' he sneers. 'I moved the Keep Out sign. The minute you jumped the ditch you went over the camp boundary. Oops.'

'That's not fair!' Jess shouts. 'You're playing a game where the rules keep changing.'

'Not only are you going to stop trying to trip me up, but you're going to do exactly as I say from now on. Or Fisher sees this. Rule twenty-five, isn't it? No going off camp or Mummy and Daddy get a visit and you get detention forever. Oh dear.'

'Well you can have this back!' Jess hands him the e-reader. 'Nobody buys my friendship. Especially with something you can't even put a special bookmark in.'

'And you can have these too.' I take off the trainers, rip off the leather bracelet, and throw the sunglasses on his bed.

'As if I care.' Zac shrugs.

Stupidly, I do. He duped me with trainers, and money, and fake coolness. But mostly lies, and I can't believe I fell for them.

COMPOSITION OF ZAC

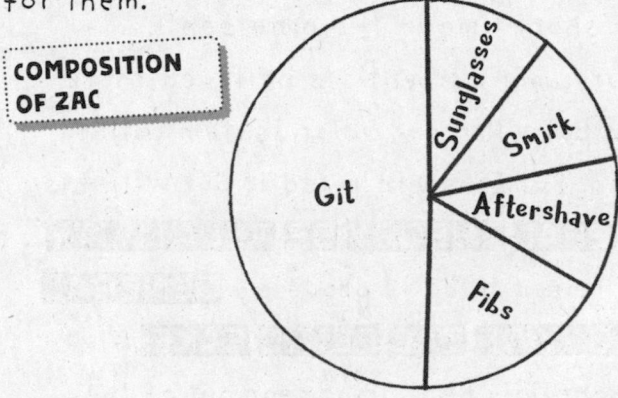

A diagram I have to draw in my mind because, to top it all, my notebook has gone missing.

I slump on my bunk bed just as Liam walks in our room.

'Stanlington,' he says, his hands cupped over his ears. 'I never thought being a deer would come in handy, but I just heard every word of that. I don't think I like super-dares any more. I think it's time for . . . splans.'

COOL-O-METER

SUPERCOOL

CHILLING OUT

NO SWEAT

IN THE SHADE

COLD FEET

ON THIN ICE

LUKEWARM

HOT AND BOTHERED

SWEATING BUCKETS

TOTAL MELTDOWN

⤷ WEAKNESSES

For a short time in the nineteenth century, many scientists believed there was a planet in our solar system called Vulcan. But Einstein ruled it out with his GENERAL THEORY OF RELATIVITY.

All I need to do is prove my GENERAL THEORY OF ZAC BEING FAKE, and hopefully he'll disappear out of the universe too.

'He's playing Monopoly,' Jess says as we head to breakfast. 'He just bought Mayfair and put three hotels on it, whilst we got sent to jail without passing Go.'

'It's obvious what we've got to do next,' Idris agrees. 'One of us has to get Zac's phone so we can destroy the evidence.'

'I don't know if you've ever seen *The Wizard of Oz*,' Jess says. 'But that's

like saying *BRING ME THE WITCH'S*
BROOMSTICK. We'd literally have to melt
him to get access to it.'

'Well, I'm up for it if you are?'

'Whatever you're planning . . .' Liam
catches us up, hitting his head on the wind
chimes. 'Count me in. His stupid trainers
don't even fit me. Gave me three blisters.'

I gasp, and everyone turns to look at me.

'It's all right, Stanlington, I've got
plasters,' Liam smiles, as we line up for
vegan porridge.

But it's not about blisters. It's about the
kitchen raid for baguettes. It's suddenly
dawned on me I had a chance to stop
Liam getting caught, as I flashback to the
figure tiptoeing through the toadstools,
walking straight into some wind chimes.
Zac would *NEVER* have hit his head on
them—he's too short. Unlike Liam.

I feel the urge to tell him everything as
we find a table next to Fred and Flossie,
but the words are stuck in my throat.

COOL-O-METER

SUPERCOOL

CHILLING OUT

NO SWEAT

IN THE SHADE

COLD FEET

ON THIN ICE

LUKEWARM

HOT AND BOTHERED

SWEATING BUCKETS

TOTAL MELTDOWN

'Um . . . ergh . . . I . . .'

'What's the matter, mate-bro?' and he looks at me with his Liam eyes and I spurt out an apology.

'I'm-really-sorry-we-thought-it-was-Zac-but-it-was-you-in-a-zombie-mask.'

'Eh?'

'We were trying to set up Zac. In the kitchens. I had no idea it was you. But I should have. I'm sorry.'

'Woah. I'm like . . . impressed you tried to do that . . . but a bit angry you got me caught. Sort of . . . impangry.' He scratches his head. 'Zac said I should go cos I could reach the tall cupboards.'

'He knew what we were up to,' Jess says. 'That's why he sent you in his place.'

'He's not just a genius. He's an EVIL genius. An EVILENIUS.'

'He's also setting up a super-dare for the last night and thinks you're going to do it. I overheard him talking,' I say. 'That's why I joined The Dogs, only I got carried away with trainer power and sunglasses.'

'Easily done. But I got Jess caught with the catapult. Think we all owe each other some sorrys.'

Suddenly, Billie Keegan walks up with armfuls of stuff and dumps it in front of Flossie.

'Look, Defective Flossie, I found all your unicorn fings. Someone hidden them in a place only I could find.' She grins. 'Anyone in the world would want me for a friend now.'

'That's a bit bananas.' She frowns, staring at it through her magnifying glass. 'I was sure it was Stan.'

I choke on my porridge.

'Fank you, Billie Keegan.' She gets up and shakes her hand. 'You can have one of my unicorn face masks as a reward. And you CAN be my friend, but not my bestest; that's Fred. And you really must lay off the stomping.'

'I will. Can we eat strawberry laces now?'

'Easy, tiger, I gotta finish my porridge

SUPERCOOL

CHILLING OUT

NO SWEAT

IN THE SHADE

COLD FEET

ON THIN ICE

COOL-O-METER

LUKEWARM

HOT AND BOTHERED

SWEATING BUCKETS

TOTAL MELTDOWN

first. And then we can play unicorns too.'

She skips off, without a hint of stomp.

Flossie leans forward: 'I fink Billie stole it all really. She wanted to be my friend, but, between you and me, was a bit rubbish at it.'

'Not everyone would have given her a unicorn face mask,' I say, relieved to no longer be a suspect.

'Yes, I know,' she sighs. 'But she's a good thiever and that might come in handy.'

Idris stares at me: 'Are you thinking what I'm thinking?'

'I'm thinking this vegan porridge is disgusting.'

'Well, that's true, but what I'm actually thinking is—a good thief is exactly what we need to get hold of Zac's phone.'

'I see what you're saying.' Flossie stands up on her chair. 'But before my team gets involved, I need to know everyfing—Zac's movements and weaknesses.'

'How old is she?' Liam whispers.

'Never underestimate a small-year-old.'

Jess pats his shoulder.

'We'll have all the information by the end of the day, Defective McGregor,' I promise, though I have no idea if I can promise it at all. 'Meet under the reading tree later for a splans update.'

Mr Fisher looks like he's been at one with nature again, even after a break from camp, as he enters the Portal Cabin hugging a coffee. 'Mentors, pick an animal and help the class put together a life-cycle chart.'

He waves at the flip chart.

'This would be the bestest day of my entire life if I didn't have to do stupid writing.' Fred kicks his chair leg. 'School work smells of grey; the wood smells of rainbows.'

'Let's get it over with. Frog or butterfly?'

'Snail.' He pouts, pretending to write on the worksheet. 'Angus gets born a slug, finds a shell with an A, magics into

COOL-O-METER

SUPERCOOL

CHILLING OUT

NO SWEAT

IN THE SHADE

COLD FEET

ON THIN ICE

LUKEWARM

HOT AND BOTHERED

SWEATING BUCKETS

TOTAL MELTDOWN

a butterfly, makes honey and dies. I'm
finished, can I go now?'

He's not the only one going off-topic,
as I draw up a life cycle of my own:

THE LIFE CYCLE OF ZAC CASSIDY

Amoeba multiplies and
Zac is born

Zac the Amoeba
evolves into a bigger
amoeba that gets
eleven pairs of
trainers he doesn't
deserve

Zac the Amoeba is
fully grown but still
one of the simplest
organisms that has
ever lived on Earth

Zac the Amoeba adapts to
its environment by wearing
sunglasses indoors

We even have time to do the correct
topic work because Mr Fisher keeps
nodding off. Zac takes advantage and
makes me do his work too, while waving his
phone at me. Eventually Jess has to go and

nudge Mr Fisher awake.

He gulps the rest of his coffee, and turns the page on the flip chart to show the correct answers.

Everyone gasps. Written in large red pen are the words:

FISHER IS A MORON
SIGNED ALASKA PIXIE
LEMONDROP MCGREGOR

Jess is staring straight ahead, trying to ignore the giggling and lame comments.

'LEMONDROP? OMG I WOULDN'T EVEN CALL MY GUINEA PIG THAT.'

Mr Fisher quickly flips the page. There isn't a hint of Light Salmon on his face.

As the lesson draws to a close, he asks Jess and me to stay behind. He doesn't say a word until the classroom is empty.

'It wasn't me, Sir!' Jess blurts out.

'No, it wasn't her!' I blurt a bit louder.

He puts his finger to his lips.

COOL-O-METER

SUPERCOOL

CHILLING OUT

NO SWEAT

IN THE SHADE

COLD FEET

ON THIN ICE

LUKEWARM

HOT AND BOTHERED

SWEATING BUCKETS

TOTAL MELTDOWN

'Even I know you're not so stupid as to sign your name against vandalism, Miss McGregor.' He takes a notebook out of the drawer. 'However, this was found by the flip chart, which may shed some light on the culprit.'

He flicks through the book, stops at a page, and places it in front of me.

'Brilliant Things About Alaska Pixie Lemondrop. I take it this is one of yours, Mr Fox?'

'Gulp. Yes Sir. But there's no way I—'

'You wrote ALL my names down?' Jess interrupts. 'The ones I didn't want anyone to know? How could you, Stanley? You promised!'

'I was trying to make you feel better—'

'Anyone could have seen this! And now everyone has!'

'I'm sorry. It was meant for you. But my notebook was stolen, Sir! And I'm sure I know who took it.'

I flick through it and suddenly spot a diagram I didn't do:

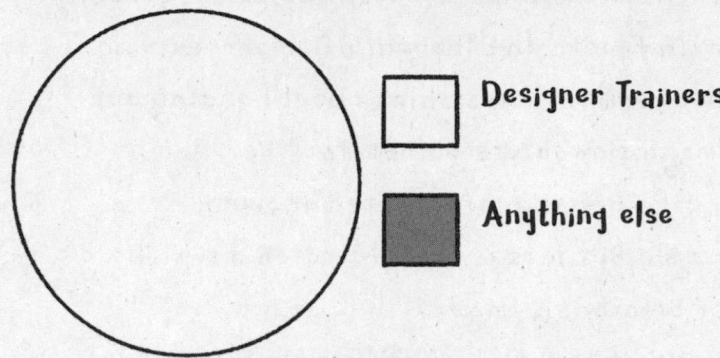

ACCEPTABLE THINGS TO WEAR ON YOUR FEET

☐ Designer Trainers

■ Anything else

COOL-O-METER

SUPERCOOL

CHILLING OUT

NO SWEAT

IN THE SHADE

COLD FEET

ON THIN ICE

LUKEWARM

HOT AND BOTHERED

SWEATING BUCKETS

TOTAL MELTDOWN

'Sir! It's obvious! It was Zac Cassidy.'

He leans in with his coffee breath and studies it.

'Hmm . . . I see.' He narrows his eyes. 'May I suggest what you learn from this is not to turn <u>EVERYTHING</u> into a diagram, Mr Fox?'

'I agree,' Jess snaps.

'But, Sir—'

'Just . . . be on your way for the next activity.'

The pond is in the middle of the wood, shaded and peaceful. Well it would be if

the small-year-olds weren't squealing with
excitement, and the parent helpers squealing
with fear at the thought of small-year-olds
near water. Rufus skips about handing out
'magical creature gatherers'.

'It's a fishing net.' Fred frowns.

'Ah! But this one might catch a whirligig
or a fairy shrimp.'

'What about sharks?' Fred leans so far
over his fringe gets dipped.

'I don't fancy your chances, puffling.'
Petra pulls him back. 'Maybe a water tiger
though—tiny beetle larvae that inject
poison into their prey, dissolving them into
soup and sucking them up.'

'That's uncalled for.' Liam wrinkles his
nose.

'That's brilliant!' Freddie's eyes are wide
with amazement, as he fishes up loads of
pondweed until I help him gently lower the net.

'Ooh! You've got a whirligig.' Rufus
grins. 'He's got two pairs of eyes, one for
using above the water and one below, and

carries a tiny air bubble so he can breathe underwater. And this pond snail has a special tube, like a snorkel.'

'SNAILS IN THE POND?' Fred laughter-cries. He's so excited all his emotions have mixed up. 'I'm going back for more!'

Idris is flicking through my notebook, muttering at Zac's diagram.

'It's obvious he wrote it on the flip chart.'

'It's not the writing of it on the flip chart that's the problem,' Jess grumbles. 'It's the writing of it IN A NOTEBOOK.'

'You can throw them away if you like.' I grab it and tear out the diagrams. 'It was a stupid idea. Here, I meant to give it you ages ago but got distracted by all the Zac stuff.'

'It's illegal to wake a sleeping bear to take its photograph? Well, that kind of makes me like Alaska a smidge more.' She puts them in her pocket. 'Anyway, I've sussed it. Zac's playing Cluedo.'

'I've sussed that you need to step away

COOL-O-METER

SUPERCOOL

CHILLING OUT

NO SWEAT

IN THE SHADE

COLD FEET

ON THIN ICE

LUKEWARM

HOT AND BOTHERED

SWEATING BUCKETS

TOTAL MELTDOWN

from the board games,' Idris tuts.

'But I'm right—Jess in the woods with the catapult, Liam in the kitchen with the baguettes, Stan in the Portal Cabin with the flip chart. He's setting us all up as the culprit so we end up hating each other. We need to set HIM up and get him with the lead piping.'

'Can we do it quick-amundo?' Liam says. 'It's only ONE DAY before the super-dare.'

'WE NEED TO KNOW HIS MOVEMENTS AND WEAKNESSES,' I repeat Flossie's line. 'Well, we know his movements. The minute everyone sits writing diaries, he'll be in his room playing games on his phone.'

'Oh look, if it isn't Little Miss Frosty and her huskies.' Maddie walks over, winding gum round her finger.

'Go away, Maddie, before we both regret it,' Jess scowls.

'What are you going to do? Turn me into a frog with your PIXIE MAGIC?' she laughs, earning a fist-bump from Zac.

'Don't tempt me.' Jess grips hold of her fishing net.

'I mean, Alaska I can just about understand, but *PIXIE LEMONDROP?*' She shakes her head. 'Did your parents mistake you for a My Little Pony?'

Jess narrows her eyes.

'It's about time you got your comeuppance, Maddie Keegan.'

'What are you going to do, blizzard me to death?'

Jess fills the net with pondweed and in one swift move brings it down over Maddie's head as she's blowing a bubble.

She's so shocked by the cold water, she doesn't even scream, as slimy weed drips off her fringe.

'You shouldn't have done that,' she says, picking up a handful of snails and launching them at Jess, who screams when they stick to her hair.

Within a matter of seconds it's chaos, as everyone starts chucking pond snails, slimy

COOL-O-METER

SUPERCOOL

CHILLING OUT

NO SWEAT

IN THE SHADE

COLD FEET

ON THIN ICE

LUKEWARM

HOT AND BOTHERED

SWEATING BUCKETS

TOTAL MELTDOWN

weed, and most probably water tigers. The parent helpers stand guard by the water with terror in their eyes.

'Stop!' Rufus shouts. 'Snails aren't weapons!'

A lump of pondweed hits him in the beard. There are gasps as it drips onto his ukulele. All falls quiet as everyone lowers their fishing nets.

'Methinks,' Petra says, 'we all need to give everyone an apology hug.'

'And then,' Rufus sniffs, fanning his eyes and trying to hold it together. 'We all need to give the SNAILS an apology hug. For that is the VERY LEAST they deserve.'

Fred rushes up to Rufus and holds his hand.

☆

After two showers I'm still convinced there are water tigers in my hair sucking my brains out. As I walk in the room to get changed, I notice a piece of paper shoved under the door with my name on it. I unfold it, and can't believe what I'm seeing: it's a pie chart, and it's filled with just the information we need: Zac's weaknesses.

Stuff Zac really doesn't like

Ghosts

Worms

Two toilet rolls being rubbed together

Thunderstorms

COOL-O-METER

SUPERCOOL

CHILLING OUT

NO SWEAT

IN THE SHADE

COLD FEET

ON THIN ICE

LUKEWARM

HOT AND BOTHERED

SWEATING BUCKETS

TOTAL MELTDOWN

⤷ A BIGGER CHART

Everyone's sat around the campfire as the sun reaches the horizon. Rufus is playing the ukulele now his beard has dried. The rest of us are huddled under the reading tree.

'I brung you something tasty.' Fred appears with his hand squished around an organic hot dog.

'Something tasty that's covered in grass. Did you drop it?'

'Nope. I was carrying it, and then I stopped carrying it.'

He blows the grass off, spraying my hot dog in Fred spit, and sits down next to Flossie and Billie. It's time for the secret splans meeting.

'So, what's the one thing you need to

catch a fly?' I ask, taking out my notebook.

'Cow plops?' Fred says, not helpfully.

'The obvious answer is <u>SPIDER WEB</u>,' I tut, holding up a page. 'Because this situation calls for a <u>SPIDER DIAGRAM!</u> Welcome to Operation CRAZE—Calculated Revenge And Zac Entrapment.'

OPERATION CRAZE

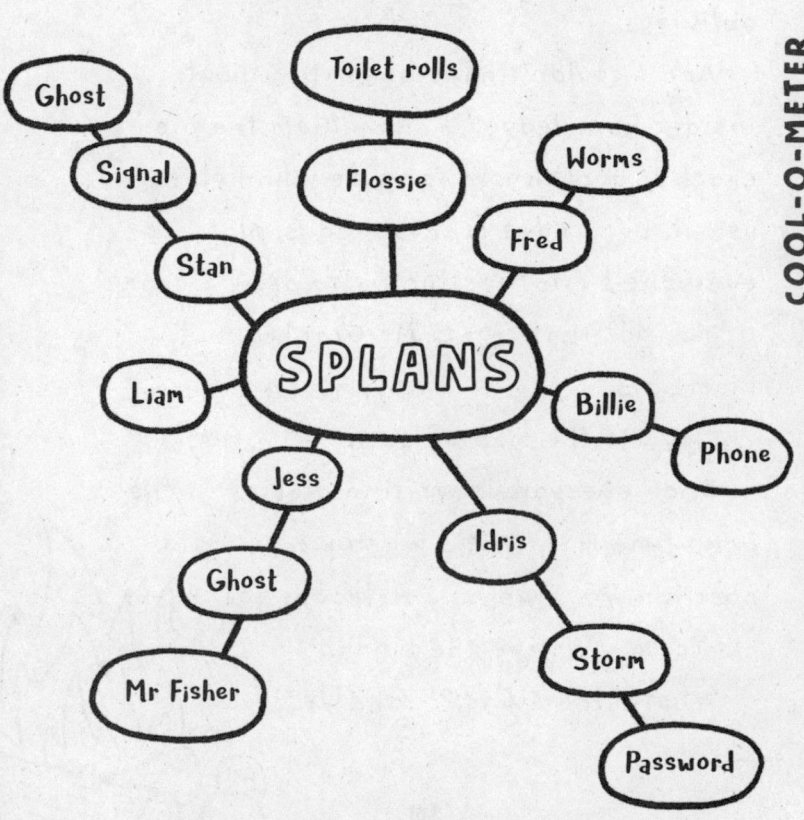

COOL-O-METER

SUPERCOOL

CHILLING OUT

NO SWEAT

IN THE SHADE

COLD FEET

ON THIN ICE

LUKEWARM

HOT AND BOTHERED

SWEATING BUCKETS

TOTAL MELTDOWN

'Woah there, Napoleon BonaChart!' Liam exclaims. 'That's a whole new level of crazy. And hang on, why's my name got nothing against it?'

'It's about playing to our strengths, while taking advantage of Zac's weaknesses, and we each have a role to play,' I explain. 'There'll be a special part for you.'

Except there isn't because Liam's mainly oblivious.

'And I couldn't have done it without insider knowledge.' I show them the pie chart. 'I don't know for sure who helped us out, but I have my suspicions. Not everyone's first instinct is to draw a chart.'

'You got that right, Sir Graph-a-Lot,' Liam says.

I lay out the map of camp.

'Once everyone's writing diaries in the Downtime Hut, that's when we get into position. As soon as Zac leaves for his room, I'll give the signal.'

'What's the signal?' asks Jess.

'An owl.'

'Just so you know,' Idris adds, 'it won't sound anything like an owl. It will sound like he's having his leg sawn off.'

'All right. Once you hear A SORT OF OWL, Flossie's team will enter the Slumber Shack here, pushing from the inside, while we draw him outside. If all goes to plan, we'll hit Zac with a triple-whammy: distraction, phone grab, set-up.'

'I'm getting too old for this,' Flossie sighs, as I fold up the plans.

'Um, Stan . . .' Jess pulls me to one side. 'Ghosts. How exactly are we supposed to pull that off?'

'With some good old-fashioned bed sheets.' I point over to the washing line. 'Also, I'll need you to take on the most dangerous part of the operation—it requires brains, quick-thinking, tree-climbing skills, and precision timing. You're the only one with all four, Jess.'

'Hope you're right—I've got a bad feeling

COOL-O-METER

SUPERCOOL
CHILLING OUT
NO SWEAT
IN THE SHADE
COLD FEET
ON THIN ICE
LUKEWARM
HOT AND BOTHERED
SWEATING BUCKETS
TOTAL MELTDOWN

about this.'

'That's what Han Solo said and he helped blow up the Death Star,' I say, imagining Zac exploding in a galaxy far, far away.

I watch Mason spinning his yo-yo on the other side of the Downtime Hut, hoping any minute now he's going to offer to write Zac's diary. Some of the Operation CRAZE crew are already in position outside waiting for the signal. I've given Liam the job of watching the rest of The Dogs so they can't ruin the splans.

'Might hang out here tonight.' Zac shrugs. 'Cause some mischief.'

He starts chucking bits of paper at people's heads and I close my eyes for a moment as I feel the splans unravelling. Mason walks over, catching the yo-yo, and putting it in his pocket. He starts sharpening a pencil that doesn't need sharpening.

'If you drew a chart,' he says out of the

corner of his mouth. 'For, like, what this exact situation needs. What would it say?'

I'm about to take a big risk. It could destroy Operation CRAZE completely. I quickly draw a pie chart and show it to him.

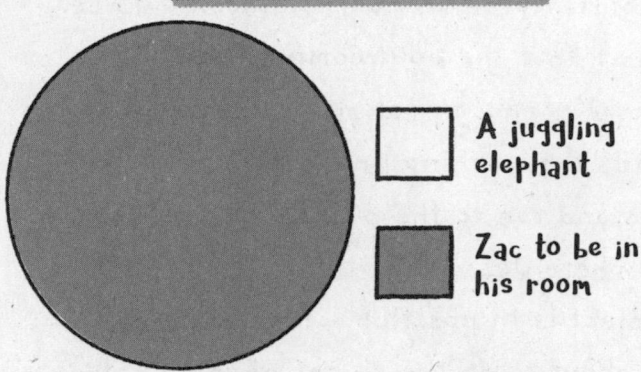

THIS EXACT SITUATION NEEDS:

□ A juggling elephant

■ Zac to be in his room

'I see,' he says, narrowing his eyes, turning and walking back over to Zac. My heart's thumping. I've put all my trust in Mason being the insider.

'Hey, Zac.' He sits down next to him. 'Guess what?'

I feel sick and take a swig of water.

'There's this brand new game, Angry Chicken Pigs. It's awesome. You should go

COOL-O-METER

SUPERCOOL
CHILLING OUT
NO SWEAT
IN THE SHADE
COLD FEET
ON THIN ICE
LUKEWARM
HOT AND BOTHERED
SWEATING BUCKETS
TOTAL MELTDOWN

play it. I'll write your diary.'

'Yeah, on second thoughts, it'll be yawnsome round here.' Zac gets up and sneaks out, and I actually say 'phew', as Mason gives me the nod.

With the teachers distracted by small-year-olds, I grab my coat and dash outside. It's dark, but the light coming from the windows is enough for me to see my way towards the washing line. I pull down the sheets and run to the bushes outside Zac's room where Jess is waiting.

'Subject is in position, Stan,' she says.

I'm about to do the signal when an actual pair of owls make a noise.

'HE-HICK . . . HOOO-OOO-OOO-OOO!'

'Wow, that was good,' she says, not taking her eyes off the patio doors.

'Um . . . thanks.'

The owls have alerted Flossie, Fred, and Billie who come trotting from the trees, covered in mud and ferns and worms and wearing unicorn face masks.

'Cover me, I'm going in,' I hear Flossie whisper, as Fred and Billie drop-roll their way to the Slumber Shack, karate-chopping the grass.

'We're relying on ninja unicorns.' I stare at Jess. 'What could possibly go wrong?'

'It's too late to back out now.' She throws the sheets over our heads, then runs off to the Downtime Hut, while I move about outside Zac's room, flapping my arms.

'WOOooooOOooo! WOOooooOOooo!'

I soon get his attention, as he opens the patio doors.

'That's meant to scare me?' he smirks. 'Lame united.'

He goes to shut the doors, but that's when three camouflaged unicorns karate kick their way into the room. Flossie jumps on the bed and starts rubbing two toilet rolls together.

COOL-O-METER

SUPERCOOL
CHILLING OUT
NO SWEAT
IN THE SHADE
COLD FEET
ON THIN ICE
LUKEWARM
HOT AND BOTHERED
SWEATING BUCKETS
TOTAL MELTDOWN

'Oh my God, I hate that!' Zac yells, putting his hands over his ears. 'Make it stop!'

But it's not about to stop as Fred jumps from one bed to the other before launching off and throwing handfuls of worms at Zac's quiff.

'Get them out! Get them out!' He staggers onto the patio, shaking his head, as Flossie quickly locks the door behind him and pulls the curtains.

I glance towards the Downtime Hut where Jess is doing a far better ghost impression than me, waving her arms about in a floaty manner. The small-year-olds are screaming as they press their noses up at the windows.

That's when the thunderstorm starts. Not a real one, but the storm on Idris's phone that he's playing from behind the bush through a speaker. A thunder crack makes Zac leap in the air, then Idris throws more worms at him just to finish him off. He yells and dashes towards the Downtime

Hut, which is exactly where another sound is coming from—the bellowing sound of a teacher with a Hot Lava Red face heading our way with a torch.

Jess has drawn Mr Fisher outside, and is now hidden up in the reading tree. As Zac runs beneath her, she flings the sheet over his head, jumps down and dives behind a bush.

'I suppose you thought that was hilarious!' Fisher yells, finally catching up and pulling off the sheet. 'Zachary Cassidy, you've caused pandemonium—how on earth are we going to calm everyone down for bedtime after your ghostly antics?'

All Zac can do is stand there open-mouthed, as he looks around for us. But we're hidden in the shadows, trying not to breathe. I can see his face. He scowls and shakes his head as it dawns on him he's been set up.

'You think this is down to me, Sir?' he snorts. 'I mean, I've been mentor of the day, like, twice.'

COOL-O-METER

SUPERCOOL

CHILLING OUT

NO SWEAT

IN THE SHADE

COLD FEET

ON THIN ICE

LUKEWARM

HOT AND BOTHERED

SWEATING BUCKETS

TOTAL MELTDOWN

'I'll take it from here, Norman.' Rufus jogs across, holding up his hand. 'I'm sure it's just a bit of artistic expression.'

'Yeah, that's exactly what it was,' Zac nods. 'Thought the kids would enjoy a laugh.'

'Oh, they're hysterical all right. It's mayhem! I think an apology is the very least you could offer.' Mr Fisher is not happy having his authority undermined.

As they disappear back to the Downtime Hut, Jess tiptoes across.

'Our splans ACTUALLY WORKED!'

'It's not over yet,' I say, knocking on the patio door three times. Billie appears, holding something. It's Zac's phone.

'We'll take payment in strawberry laces,' she says, and an exchange occurs.

'Now we need a password.' Idris starts trying different ones, while Fred and Flossie scoop up the worms and put them back in the woods.

But it's no use, Idris can't unlock it.

'I was convinced it would be super-dares.

Or trainers. Or lame united.'

'Stupid idiots,' someone says, and we spin round to see Tash ducking through the trees with Liam, as they both hit their heads on the wind chimes.

'That's a bit uncalled for—'

'No. That's the password. Stupid idiots. All one word, no caps. I've seen him type it.'

'It's one of the benefits of being tallmundous,' Liam adds. 'You can peer over shoulders.'

Tash and Liam high-five each other, and I realize Liam isn't quite as oblivious as he seems.

'Mason said you were planning something, so I offered Liam my help,' Tash says. 'We've been wanting out for ages and this is our best chance. You're not the only one who needs some evidence destroyed.'

'I'm in!' Idris says, unlocking the phone.

'Make sure you delete another video too,' Tash says. 'Me and Mason putting a unicycle in a skip. Not proud of it. It was

COOL-O-METER

SUPERCOOL

CHILLING OUT

NO SWEAT

IN THE SHADE

COLD FEET

THIN ON ICE

LUKEWARM

HOT AND BOTHERED

SWEATING BUCKETS

TOTAL MELTDOWN

Rufus's. But I'll put it right now and we'll be free of The Dogs.'

'I can help you with that, missy.' Flossie prods her. 'Cos it was <u>MY</u> skip. Been trying to solve that crime for ages. You're lucky I don't arrest you.'

Tash gulps.

It takes a few seconds to complete the task, before Billie puts the phone back where she found it.

'Stan!' Jess spins me round. 'We blew up the Death Star!'

'Yeah,' I nod, not quite believing we did it. 'Boom.'

We're about to high-five when Fred comes running out from the woods, tears streaking his cheeks like snail trails.

'Stan!' he blubs. 'Stan!'

'Woah, Fred, what is it?'

'I've lost Angus! I can't find him everywhere!'

⤷ THE GREAT BIG STAN CHALLENGE

Apollo astronauts had to leave some things behind before blasting back home to Earth. Moon buggies, golf balls, cameras, and a telescope were all left on the surface of the Moon, along with ninety-six bags of poop and wee. Fred's leaving some of his wee behind in Whispering Woods because he thinks scenting the trees will lead Angus back to him.

'If anything, Fred, that's going to put him right off.'

We've been hunting for Angus since early o'clock, despite me drawing a Snail Chart on why woods are better than pockets:

COOL-O-METER

SUPERCOOL
CHILLING OUT
NO SWEAT
IN THE SHADE
COLD FEET
ON THIN ICE
LUKEWARM
HOT AND BOTHERED
SWEATING BUCKETS
TOTAL MELTDOWN

WHY WOODS ARE BETTER THAN POCKETS

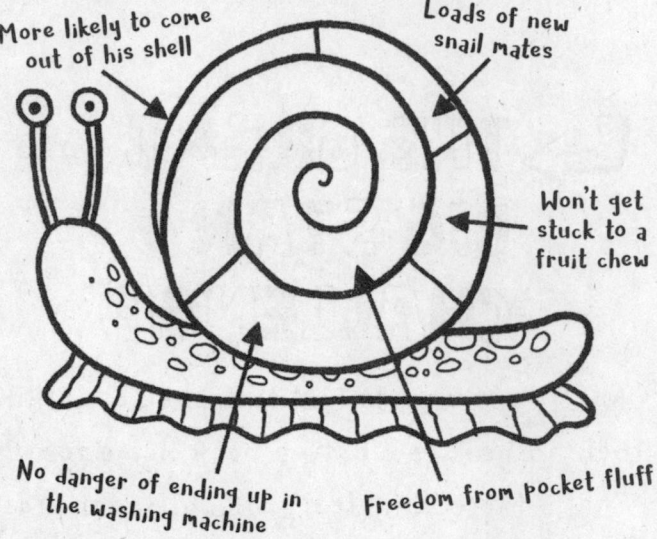

More likely to come out of his shell

Loads of new snail mates

Won't get stuck to a fruit chew

No danger of ending up in the washing machine

Freedom from pocket fluff

I also remind him of what Rufus said: 'Now he's outside he can grow a healthy shell.'

'But I feel as sad as a wood meece without its tail,' he sniffs, dragging his feet.

I give him a hug and promise everyone will look out for Angus—today is the GREAT BIG SCHOOL CHALLENGE, and whichever school wins gets to sleep out under the stars tonight. A fact Larkfield are well aware of, because they're already cramming up on nature facts as we gather round the toadstools.

Zac struts up to me in his Earth Whisperers and starts clapping slowly.

'Not a bad attempt,' he smirks. 'But the whole ghost thing was lame united. I easily got out of my punishment—charmed Mrs Fry with my brownie recipe. Thank God it's the last day, and time for the biggest super-dare ever—'

'Morning, Zachary,' Petra interrupts. 'Fancy helping me set up?'

'Course, Petra, nothing I'd rather do,' he lies and squirms off in his squirmy way.

'He's way too calm,' Tash whispers. 'He can't know about his phone. But when he does, he'll be like a dormant volcano that's suddenly not dormant.'

'And it won't matter. We're free of him,' Mason sighs, as though a weight has been lifted off his very sturdy shoulders.

'I don't know if you've ever seen THE WIZARD OF OZ,' Jess says, 'but this is like that bit where they melt the witch and all the flying monkeys switch sides to

COOL-O-METER

SUPERCOOL

CHILLING OUT

NO SWEAT

IN THE SHADE

COLD FEET

ON THIN ICE

LUKEWARM

HOT AND BOTHERED

SWEATING BUCKETS

TOTAL MELTDOWN

celebrate.'

'It's also like the Ancient Greeks,' I say.

'Bear with him.' Liam rolls his eyes. 'It'll be about space.'

'They believed the Earth was the centre of the solar system, and everything, including the Sun, revolved around it. Until a load of brilliant astronomers worked together to show it wasn't. The Sun was.'

'So you're the Sun and we revolve around you now?' Tash frowns.

'No. I'M not the Sun. The Sun's up there. Get a life and revolve around that.'

'Oh, like a kind of Planet Tash? Cool.'

'By the way,' I whisper to Mason. 'It was you wasn't it? That did the pie chart?'

'Was it alright? I wasn't sure if—'

'It was MORE than alright. We couldn't have done it without you. But how did you know we needed his weaknesses?'

'Deer ears,' he says, flapping them. 'I was thinking . . . might try something more complex next time.'

I notice he's not spinning the yo-yo any more.

'Draw on those inner animals today, pufflings.' Petra pushes her glasses up her nose. 'For I spy with my inner eye . . . a sea lion—energetic, cheeky, and agile.'

She points to Billie, who claps her hands.

'Oh, and a warthog—bit cranky, overly reliant on aggression, but otherwise ultra-intelligent.'

She pats Mr Fisher on the arm while he thinks it over.

'Cast an eyeball back to everything you've learned,' Rufus says. 'Be brilliant, yeah? Every correct answer earns a golden pine cone—so let's free that knowledge.'

The parent helpers seem enthusiastic, but that might be because it's the last day. Not surprisingly, most of the activities play to Larkfield's strengths, because it's a competition. They win pine cones for

COOL-O-METER

SUPERCOOL
CHILLING OUT
NO SWEAT
IN THE SHADE
COLD FEET
ON THIN ICE
LUKEWARM
HOT AND BOTHERED
SWEATING BUCKETS
TOTAL MELTDOWN

identifying trees, birds, and Rufus's lame animal impressions.

'Ah, but do they know the intricacies of the water cycle?' Fisher taps his nose.

Yes they do and they win that round too, even though it's been our main topic at school since forever. It's only thanks to Fred we win any pine cones at all, when he correctly identifies minibeasts and does a vivid impression of a devil's coach horse.

By lunchtime we've lost the scavenger hunt because we try to find Angus instead, and apparently you can't bring back the same eight items.

SCAVENGER HUNT

snail — Something round

snail — Something fragile

snail — Something smooth

snail — Something slimy

snail — Something shiny

snail — Something special

snail — Something brown

snail — Something squidgy

'I've been Stanalysing the situation all morning, and unless there's a miracle, we're definitely going to lose,' I say as we munch our artisan packed lunches by the stream.

'You need to quit the Stan words or I won't be responsible for my actions,' Jess grumbles.

I watch Rufus walk over to Fred and offer him a biscuit. For a moment I think he's going to refuse, but he quickly scoffs the lot, dropping crumbs everywhere.

'Bit of water on that, you've got yourself a magical biscuit tree.' Rufus covers them over with his foot.

'Really truly?'

'Never know,' he winks. 'Now, it's time for the final challenge—tracking. But instead of finding animals, you need to find me—you'll be great at this, Fred.'

'I'll be the bestest, bravest Fred Danger I can possibly be! I shall karate kick trees, chop down rabbits, and eat monkeys.'

'Why don't you try being the best

COOL-O-METER

SUPERCOOL
CHILLING OUT
NO SWEAT
IN THE SHADE
COLD FEET
ON THIN ICE
LUKEWARM
HOT AND BOTHERED
SWEATING BUCKETS
TOTAL MELTDOWN

FREDDIE FOX you can possibly be?' Rufus suggests. 'Bravery isn't all about ladybird beards and canoeing off cliffs. It can be quieter than that. Like letting Angus go cos you'll know he'll be happier.'

'What about wrestling bears and dangling from jelly-hopters?'

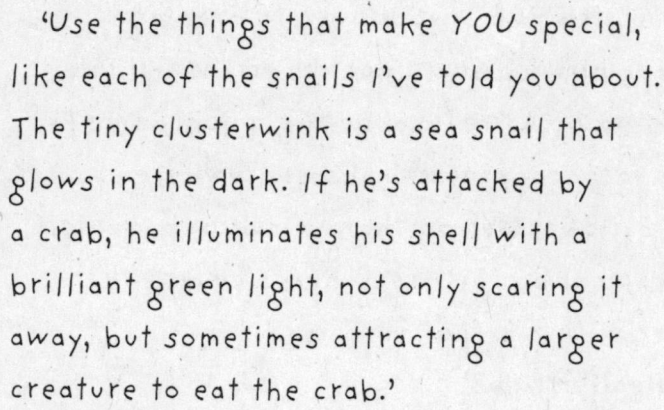

'Use the things that make YOU special, like each of the snails I've told you about. The tiny clusterwink is a sea snail that glows in the dark. If he's attacked by a crab, he illuminates his shell with a brilliant green light, not only scaring it away, but sometimes attracting a larger creature to eat the crab.'

Fred gasps.

'I fink clusterwinks are my favourites of all.'

'Me too. Right, time to hide!' Rufus doffs his flat cap and sprints into the woods, or at least tries to in his tight skinny jeans.

Fred digs his hands into the mud and wipes it across his face, tucks leaves in his hair and shorts, then stands on a tree stump to address us all.

'EXCUSE ME!' he yells, as several birds take flight and move somewhere less full of Fred. 'FLINT DANGER ALWAYS SAYS—'

But he stops, thinks, and lowers his voice to almost normal.

'Petra and Rufus always say when you're tracking fings you need deer ears and fox feet. We need to move slowly and creepily, but most of all foxily, like a Freddie Fox. Everyone tune into your senses, and look out for Rufus's droppings.'

'I hope that won't be necessary.' I scrunch my nose up.

We head into the woods as the sky starts to cloud over. While Fred checks for bent blades of grass and tiptoes around looking for signs of footprints, I spot Zac and Maddie arguing in the trees. I cup my ears.

'You think I don't know what your dumb little sister did?'

'Leave Billie out of this. She's NOT dumb.'

COOL-O-METER

SUPERCOOL

CHILLING OUT

NO SWEAT

IN THE SHADE

COLD FEET

ON THIN ICE

LUKEWARM

HOT AND BOTHERED

SWEATING BUCKETS

TOTAL MELTDOWN

'I bet you had something to do with it.'

'No I didn't, but I wish I did!' Maddie wipes her fringe from her eyes. 'I've had it with The Dogs. I quit!'

'I don't need you anyway. You only hang out with me cos you've got no friends.'

'You haven't got any either!' She stomps off.

Zac spots me and struts over.

'Look at you lot, tiptoeing about like swots.' He lifts his sunglasses. 'You could easily win—there's loads of pine cones at the hut. You only need about ten and Camford Primary could win a competition for once.'

'We don't want to cheat,' Liam says. 'And it's fun, anyway.'

'Fun if you're a loser,' he sneers. 'I'll help you get them if you want. I'm not bothered about Larkfield winning. They're all saddos. Just think—you'll be able to do all that lame star-gazing stuff.'

I know we need a miracle to win, but this wasn't quite what I was looking for.

'Anyway, it's up to you. All I'm interested in is the biggest super-dare ever. And I reckon it's your turn, S-Dog.'

'You can't make me do anything,' I say. 'NOT ANY MORE.'

'Oh dear.' He turns up the collar on his leather jacket and the wind actually kicks in, ruffling his quiff. 'Just when you think you've won. STUPID IDIOTS was a clue, you stupid idiots. I have eleven pairs of trainers. You think I only had ONE phone?'

He pulls out another and starts playing the clip of us jumping the ditch.

'He's playing chess,' Jess says through gritted teeth. 'We thought we had checkmate, only we didn't.'

'You are my puppets. I am the puppet-master,' Zac laughs like a maniac. 'You will do whatever I say. Forever. Or shall I go and show Norman you lot trekking over the boundary?'

'You tricked us into doing that!'

COOL-O-METER

SUPERCOOL

CHILLING OUT

NO SWEAT

IN THE SHADE

COLD FEET

ON THIN ICE

LUKEWARM

HOT AND BOTHERED

SWEATING BUCKETS

TOTAL MELTDOWN

'You're so easy to trick, it's unbelievable. Anyway, what's the problem?' He shrugs. 'You can fill your rucksack with pine cones AND do the biggest super-dare ever. Think that's a yes, isn't it, S-Dog? Because you've literally got no choice. Rule number twenty-five—Norman gives you detention to infinity and beyond!'

Liam steps forward.

'Not Stan. Me. I got us into this mess, I'll get us out. But only if you leave us alone. You need to promise you'll stop the blackmail if I do this.'

'Fine. Whatever.'

'No Liam!' I shout. 'Don't go! There has to be another way.'

Before I can stop him, he runs off the path into the woods with Zac.

'Maybe it's time to tell the teachers,' Jess says, shivering. It's starting to get chilly under the canopy, as fat raindrops splosh the ground and the woodland's earthy smell grows richer.

'Yeah. I don't like this one bit.'

Maddie appears, holding Billie's hand.

'It's something to do with the scarecrow,' she says, hiding her red eyes beneath her fringe. 'That's all I know. And he's going to blame it on Liam.'

'Like we're going to start trusting you,' Jess snorts.

'Fine. Don't believe me. I'm not even in the stupid gang any more.'

'It's true, Jess,' I say.

'He shouted at Billie for taking the phone.' Maddie hugs her sister closer. 'And, well, that crosses a line.'

'And calling me all those names doesn't?' Jess snaps.

Maddie chews her lip. They stare at each other, as lightning flickers around us.

'It's just, I—'

Suddenly an almighty thunderclap makes us jump. In the distance we hear whistles blowing. The parent helpers are calling us back: there's going to be a storm. I grab

Fred's hand and we start heading towards camp, but Zac runs out of nowhere, shoving my arm as he races past. He's caked in mud, his eyes are wide—he's terrified.

'Hey!' I call after him.

But he keeps running. I catch him up, grab his jacket sleeve and spin him around.

'Where's Liam?'

'Get off me.' He shakes free of my grip.

'WHERE IS HE?'

'You say I was anywhere near and I'll show them the film!' he calls back, disappearing into the trees, as the woodland flashes with light again.

My mind is filled with thoughts: Zac was covered in stinky mud. There's only one place Liam could be.

'Go get help, Jess. Take Fred and Flossie.'

'I want to come with you.' Freddie tugs my sleeve. 'I can tiptoe like a fox.'

'Listen, Fred.' I grab his shoulders. 'I need you to use your outdoor voice. Find Petra and Rufus.'

'Can I shout louder than I've ever shouted before?'

'Oh yes.'

They run off together and I'm alone in the wood, shivering as the rain lashes down.

Dad always says fear is like a bruised banana. You can smell it a mile away, nobody wants to go near it, but more often than not it looks worse than it actually is. Nevertheless, I'm not happy about peeling it.

I take out Gran's red wool and tie it to a tree. I put on the head torch, and shine it into the woods. There's no choice but to go off the path. I'm not sure I can do this.

And then I remember those cool montages they have in movies where the hero remembers all the good times they've had, to help them get through the bad times. I think of Liam and all the stuff we've done, set to a great piece of rock music.

COOL-O-METER

SUPERCOOL

CHILLING OUT

NO SWEAT

IN THE SHADE

COLD FEET

THIN ON ICE

LUKEWARM

HOT AND BOTHERED

SWEATING BUCKETS

TOTAL MELTDOWN

BEST MATE MEMORY MONTAGE

ARGUING ABOUT 'MOON CHEESE' NOT BEING AN ACTUAL THING

CYCLING IN THE RAIN TO GET BURRITOS

GO-KARTING DOWN HALLIWAY HILL WITH NO BRAKES

INVENTING FOOD DAYS LIKE CRISP SANDWICH AWARENESS, AND NATIONAL HUG A PIZZA DAY

COVERING OURSELVES IN BEANBAG CONTENTS AND PRETENDING WE WERE YETIS

DRESSING UP AS HARRY AND RON ON OUR FIRST WORLD BOOK DAY EVEN THOUGH WE DIDN'T PLAN IT

TRYING TO BREAK THE WORLD RECORD OF ARMPIT FARTS IN 30 SECONDS

THE BEST SNOWBALL FIGHT EVER IN THE HISTORY OF THE WORLD UNTIL WE BROKE MR FISHER'S WINDOW

I unwind the wool behind me, hurrying into the woods and try to remember the way, but the trees all seem the same. I double back, and pretty soon I'm lost.

I hear Fred's voice echoing in my head, 'TIPTOE LIKE A FOX', and walk as lightly as I can while the rain bounces off my head. Focus. There's the hollowed oak, probably as old as the Spanish Armada. I fight my way through the brambles, climb over a fallen tree, and leap over ditches. I spot trampled grass and the imprint of a trainer.

'Liam!' I shout, cupping my ears as the rumble of thunder goes right through me.

And then I see it. Shining like a piece of gold. A hula hoop. Then another, and another. It's a trail! I follow it, and sure enough it brings me out under a prickly holly bush to the hut. The door's open, but there's no sign of anyone inside.

'Over here!'

I run down the ditch and up to the fence.

COOL-O-METER

SUPERCOOL

CHILLING OUT

NO SWEAT

IN THE SHADE

COLD FEET

ON THIN ICE

LUKEWARM

HOT AND BOTHERED

SWEATING BUCKETS

TOTAL MELTDOWN

Liam's in the middle of the bog, a rucksack
on his back, soaked through.

'I s-s-sacrificed my H-H-Hula Hoops,
man-bro,' he shivers. 'So you'd find me.'

'I know.'

'He . . . r-r-ran off.'

'I'll get you out.' I climb over the fence,
and try to walk towards him, but rain
has turned it into a swamp. Lightning
illuminates the shadows for a split second,
and I notice the scarecrow is missing.

'Oh my God. Where's the—'

'It's OK, Stan. It's on the ground. Zac
wanted to drag it back to camp and scare
you all tonight when you were star-gazing.'

'Blimey. That would have worked.'

'We were trying to pull it across when I
got s-s-stuck. And then he—'

'Ran off. The thunderstorm. He hates
them.'

'And he's wearing Earth Whisperers,
o-o-obvs.'

'See if you can crawl towards me,' I shout

through the rain. 'Find your inner sloth,
like you're trying to reach the TV remote.'

'I can't. My feet are w-w-wedged.'

I pick up a fallen branch and stretch out
to him, but my arms are too short. I run
back to the hut, slipping on the mud, bang
open the door and start rifling through the
crates, but they're empty. I turn round and
spot rope hooked on the door. Once I'm back
through the fence, that's when I hear the
haunting, creaking sound.

'What the heck was that?' Liam looks
petrified.

'Don't worry, grab this.' I fling the rope,
but the wind and rain lash it back.

'Well I AM worrying,' he shouts. 'What if . . .
Stan, what if they really do come to life?'

Then comes the grunting, beastly noise. The
sort of noise that makes you pull the duvet up
round your ears after watching a scary film.

'Stan! I can see my life flashing before
my eyes, and it's all Hula Hoops! S-s-save
yourself!'

COOL-O-METER

SUPERCOOL

CHILLING OUT

NO SWEAT

IN THE SHADE

COLD FEET

ON THIN ICE

LUKEWARM

HOT AND BOTHERED

SWEATING BUCKETS

TOTAL MELTDOWN

'Hey . . . remember that time we got burritos?'

'Yeah,' he half smiles.

'It was raining heavier than this. We can do it, Liam.' I throw the rope again and this time he grabs it. 'Hold on.'

I try to pull him out, but my hands are too wet. As the clouds crash above, all I want to do is run. But my **LOYALTY SCALES** say different.

'Something's coming . . .' Liam whimpers, looking behind me.

I spin round and see someone jump the fence. Someone with a plank under his arm, which he lays over the bog. Then he grabs the rope and pulls Liam to drier ground.

'Mr Fisher!' Liam gasps, having never been happy to see him until right now.

'Quick thinking on the wool, Stan,' he says. 'And thank Fred when you see him. Got a good set of lungs on him, hasn't he?'

'Um, yes Sir.'

'Ouch! My leg—think it's broken,' Liam sniffles, grabbing his shin.

'It's just a graze.' Mr Fisher grabs blankets from the hut and wraps us in them.

'Thanks, Sir, and I realize we were beyond the camp boundary, but—' Liam stops mid-sentence as the eerie creaking suddenly grows louder. 'The scarecrow! It's coming to life!'

'That's no scarecrow,' Rufus says, finally catching up. 'It's the beech trees. Their branches are rubbing together in the wind. Sounds like a ship on the high seas, yeah?'

'But there's definitely SOMETHING in the woods.'

'There is.' Rufus points. 'Look.'

SUPERCOOL

CHILLING OUT

NO SWEAT

IN THE SHADE

COLD FEET

ON THIN ICE

COOL-O-METER

LUKEWARM

HOT AND BOTHERED

SWEATING BUCKETS

TOTAL MELTDOWN

We both turn around. At the fence, snorting and grunting, is a massive pig.

'You got yourself stuck in a pig wallow. The farmer tried to warn you with a Keep Out sign and the scarecrow. Hey! Where IS the scarecrow?'

Rufus tries to hop over the fence but fails because of his tight skinny jeans.

'Leave it to me.' Mr Fisher vaults it in one, and walks along the plank, hoisting the scarecrow onto his shoulder. 'We'll have to fix it up or the farmer won't be happy.'

'What were you doing—trying to drag it to camp?' Rufus tuts. 'Cos that's totally not cool, guys.'

'It wasn't us!' Liam shouts.

'Hmmm, I think we need a little chat-dot-com,' Rufus says, having seen what's inside the rucksack.

'Oh yes. We need a chat all right,' Mr Fisher agrees.

We make it back to the toadstools when Fred rushes up and hugs my legs.

'I was being a clusterwink and flashing my torch and shouting the loudest I could.'

'You were brilliant, Fred.' I grab his hand, then spot the crowd waiting to greet us, a crowd which gasps when it spots the raggedy scarecrow on Fisher's shoulder. They gasp even louder when Rufus empties the rucksack and a load of pine cones fall to the ground.

'So, dudes, trying to cheat, were we?'

'It's all his fault!' Liam points to Zac, who's stood smirking now he's all dry and warm beneath an umbrella.

'It was nothing to do with me. I mean, we were winning—why would I want to cheat?' he shrugs. 'And Liam wanted to steal the farmer's scarecrow and frighten everyone. Obviously I refused, I mean, that's totally literally breaking the rules.'

'You liar! You <u>MADE</u> me! And when I got stuck you ran off. Didn't even look back.'

'I came to get help, L-Dog. First thing I did was find Stan. I'd have gone with him

COOL-O-METER

SUPERCOOL
CHILLING OUT
NO SWEAT
IN THE SHADE
COLD FEET
ON THIN ICE
LUKEWARM
HOT AND BOTHERED
SWEATING BUCKETS
TOTAL MELTDOWN

if I hadn't twisted my ankle.' Zac fake winces, holding his foot.

'When are you EVER going to stop lying?' I shout.

'I'm not the liar here. I'm an excellent student. I know what a bullfinch is and everything.'

'Sure you do Zachary, we're not blaming you—'

'If I may interject for a moment, Rufus.' Mr Fisher steps forward. 'Not many people know this, but I'm a member of the Camford Amateur Dramatic Society. My Bottom received a standing ovation. So trust me when I say, I know a good act when I see one. And you, Zachary Cassidy, are one of the finest.'

'Woah. Let's just rewind for a sec, shall we?' Rufus puts his hand up. 'Larkfield's exemplary record speaks for itself—one of our students would never get mixed up in this kind of behaviour.'

'I've had enough of this.' Idris marches up to the teachers and takes out his phone. 'I realize this is against the rules, Mr Fisher, but you really need to see this.'

He presses play.

'YOU ARE MY PUPPETS. I AM THE PUPPET-MASTER,' ZAC LAUGHS LIKE A MANIAC. 'YOU WILL DO WHATEVER I SAY. FOREVER. OR SHALL I GO AND SHOW NORMAN YOU LOT TREKKING OVER THE BOUNDARY?'

'YOU TRICKED US INTO DOING THAT!'

'YOU'RE SO EASY TO TRICK, IT'S UNBELIEVABLE. ANYWAY, WHAT'S THE PROBLEM? YOU CAN FILL YOUR RUCKSACK WITH PINE CONES AND DO THE BIGGEST SUPER-DARE EVER. THINK THAT'S A YES, ISN'T IT, S-DOG? BECAUSE YOU'VE LITERALLY GOT NO CHOICE. RULE NUMBER TWENTY-FIVE—NORMAN GIVES YOU DETENTION TO INFINITY AND BEYOND!'

COOL-O-METER

SUPERCOOL

CHILLING OUT

NO SWEAT

IN THE SHADE

COLD FEET

ON THIN ICE

LUKEWARM

HOT AND BOTHERED

SWEATING BUCKETS

TOTAL MELTDOWN

'NOT STAN. ME. I GOT US INTO THIS
MESS, I'LL GET US OUT. BUT ONLY IF
YOU LEAVE US ALONE. YOU NEED TO
PROMISE YOU'LL STOP THE BLACKMAIL
IF I DO THIS.'

'FINE. WHATEVER.'

'NO LIAM! DON'T GO! THERE HAS TO BE
ANOTHER WAY.'

Idris stops the video. Everyone's staring
at Zac.

'You're going down for a long time,
mister!' Flossie shouts, taking out her
handcuffs.

'It's OK, Flossie,' Mr Fisher says. 'We'll
deal with this.'

'That's a whole lot of disappointment,
Zachary.' Rufus shakes his head.

'I spy with my inner eye . . .' Petra
steps forward. 'A crocodile—enterprising,
ruthless in nature, with a self-interest in
its survival.'

'Oh come on, it was just a bit of fun,' he

laughs nervously. 'Tell them it wasn't ALL my fault, L-Dog? Mason? Tash?'

'I flippin' hate yo-yos!' Mason takes it out of his pocket and smashes it to the ground.

'And you can be your own look-out,' Tash says. 'Cos my eyes belong to me!'

'Whatever. I've still got Mads on my team.'

'No.' She takes hold of Billie's hand. 'THIS is my team.'

'The Dogs are no more,' Liam says, standing close to me. 'You're on your own, sad and lonely—slonely. And it's all your fault, foe-bro. And, by the way, MY NAME'S LIAM.'

'That's right, run back to Chart Geek and his lame splans. See if I care.'

'You leave my big bruvver alone!' Fred steps forward, shining his torch in Zac's face.

'Shut up, squirt! You think I don't know it was you who threw worms at me. Hey, hang on a minute, isn't this one of your stupid pets?'

He points to the ground in front of him.

'Angus isn't it? Oh dear. You should have

COOL-O-METER

SUPERCOOL
CHILLING OUT
NO SWEAT
IN THE SHADE
COLD FEET
ON THIN ICE
LUKEWARM
HOT AND BOTHERED
SWEATING BUCKETS
TOTAL MELTDOWN

kept a tighter hold on him.'

He lifts up his leg, and smashes it down on the ground with a crunch.

'NOOOOOOOOOOOOOOOOOOOOOOOOOOOOOOO OOOOOOOOOOOOOOOOOOOOOOOOOOOOOOOO OOOOOOOOOOOOOOOOOOOOOOOOOOOOOOOO OOOO!' Fred screams.

'You utter git!' I go to run forward but Idris and Jess hold me back.

'As much as I'd love you to punch him, he's not worth it, Stan,' Jess says, as the teachers lead him away. 'Besides, Fred needs you.'

Fred is knelt on the ground, tears streaming down his face which is already wet from the rain. I gather him up in a hug. Of all the things Zac Cassidy has done, this one hurts the most.

STARS AND SNAILS

The astronauts on the Apollo 13 mission were supposed to walk on the Moon. In the end they could only watch the lunar surface as they circled it—their mission was to get home safely.

I watch the rain beating the window and washing away my chances of seeing the Milky Way. We're tucked up in the Downtime Hut, where Petra and Mrs Parker have turned out the lights and set up an indoor camp. Most are sat around a tissue-paper fire lit with fairy lights, singing songs by torchlight and eating their own weight in marshmallows.

Instead of one school winning the `GREAT BIG SCHOOL CHALLENGE,`

SUPERCOOL
CHILLING OUT
NO SWEAT
IN THE SHADE
COLD FEET
ON THIN ICE
LUKEWARM
HOT AND BOTHERED
SWEATING BUCKETS
TOTAL MELTDOWN
COOL-O-METER

everyone's given individual awards,
like Best Bedtime Storyteller (Flossie
McGregor), Most Enthusiastic Deer Ears
(Mason Donovan), and Greatest Rain
Collector (Billie Keegan—even though it
was actually pee).

But the main gossip is about Zac, who's
been in The Touch Base with Rufus for the
past hour, while each of us have had to
talk to Mr Fisher.

Fred's curled up on the sofa. Nothing I do
or say can console him. Not even Flossie's
strawberry laces or the Jammie Dodgers
Mrs Fry managed to find in the kitchen.

'I should have made Angus a suit of
armour,' he sobs.

Jess walks over with Maddie, the last to
be interrogated.

'Maddie's got something she needs to tell
you.'

'I definitely don't want to hear it.'

'You really do, Stan. And especially Fred.'

Maddie sits down beside him with

something in her hand. Slowly she opens
her palm, and shines a torch on a squashed
pine cone.

'It wasn't Angus he stamped on. It was
this. Zac tricked you.'

Fred frowns as he stares at it.

'That's worse!' I shout. 'He deliberately
made Fred believe he'd killed Angus!'

'S-s-so Angus isn't deaded?' Fred's
bottom lip trembles.

'No,' Maddie says. 'And I've got something
else.'

She unfolds a drawing of a snail.

'Wow. I didn't know you could draw like
that,' Jess says.

'I can't. Zac did it.'

'I like it lotsly. Also I don't.' Fred pushes
it away.

'Can't blame you.' She shrugs. 'But it's his
way of saying sorry.'

'Still makes me want to punch him.' I
shake my head.

'Violence is not the answer, pufflings.'

SUPERCOOL

CHILLING OUT

NO SWEAT

IN THE
SHADE

COLD FEET

ON
THIN ICE

COOL-O-METER

LUKEWARM

HOT AND
BOTHERED

SWEATING
BUCKETS

TOTAL
MELTDOWN

Petra walks over. 'And anyway, a night alone with his thoughts might help. I am sensing a leopard that may want to change its spots.'

She leads Fred off to join Flossie and Billie, who are sat cutting paper snowflakes by the tissue-paper fire.

'Leopards can't change their spots,' Idris snarls. 'Everyone knows that.'

'Oh, I don't' know,' Jess says, offering marshmallows to Maddie.

'Thanks.' She wipes her fringe from her eyes. 'Me and Zac we're . . . rubbish at making friends. That's why we hung out together. He only liked me when I was mean to people. So I kept on being mean to people. Dumb, right?'

'Well, yeah.'

'Billie really likes your sister. I'm happy she found a friend. A proper one, y'know. Though she didn't go about it the right way, nicking all that unicorn stuff.'

'Flossie could see she was a good person.'

'Sorry about the Alaska thing. To be honest, it's a pretty cool name. Oh. I don't mean in, like, a polar region way. I mean, it's GOOD cool.'

'Maybe, but my name's Jess. And if you call me that again you'll get another fishing net on your head.'

'Fair enough.'

I watch Fred throw paper snowflakes in the air, which flutter back down around him.

'You came back for me, Stan-bro.' Liam punches my shoulder.

'Couldn't leave you at the mercy of wood zombies.'

He lets out a loud sob and pulls me in for a hug.

'Sorry mate. Been a right fooligan.'

'It's Zac who's been a fooligan.'

'But what you did was the coolest thing EVER. One minute longer and I'd have been pig food. Dunno how to make it up to you.'

'Go-karting down Halliway Hill might do it.'

'Y-e-a-h . . .' he says slowly, which means

COOL-O-METER

SUPERCOOL

CHILLING OUT

NO SWEAT

IN THE SHADE

COLD FEET

ON THIN ICE

LUKEWARM

HOT AND BOTHERED

SWEATING BUCKETS

TOTAL MELTDOWN

he's thinking—I can almost hear his brain clunking. He gets up and goes over to Petra, who nods and pats his arm.

'Hey pufflings!' she says. 'Liam has had a <u>BRILLIANT</u> idea. And I'm all for promoting those.'

'He has?' Jess frowns.

'Er, yeah. See my mate Stan, over there?' He points, and I blush. 'He's mad about space like I'm mad about Hula Hoops. Which is A LOT. Anyhoodle, he really wanted to see the Milky Way on this trip, but . . . what with the rain . . . so, this might be the lamest thing I've ever done, but, join in. Please . . .'

He squats down and asks to borrow a snowflake from Fred. He takes a torch and shines it up through the paper cuttings. A kaleidoscope of lights dance across the ceiling.

'Look, Stan!' Freddie shouts, as everyone grabs one and does the same. 'Twinkly stars!'

'Oh yeah,' I say, with a bit of a squeak in

my voice, and make a mental note to add it to my Best Mate Memory Montage.

'Woah! That looks like the Big Hippo constellation, doesn't it, Stan?'

'Yes. Yes it does, Liam,' I say, not wanting to tell him there's no such thing as the Big Hippo constellation.

Mrs Parker has agreed for Fred and me to sleep in the same room tonight, seeing as he's still teary over Angus.

'I think he might need your Fred Alert Kit after all,' she says.

Mason kindly offered to swap rooms, because Zac is being kept in the other Slumber Shack where a bajillion parent helpers can keep an eye on him.

'And I've always wanted to sleep in a bunk bed,' he grins.

Although the fact Liam still has loads of snacks might be something to do with it.

Even with a duvet as soft as a cloud I

COOL-O-METER

SUPERCOOL

CHILLING OUT

NO SWEAT

IN THE SHADE

COLD FEET

ON THIN ICE

LUKEWARM

HOT AND BOTHERED

SWEATING BUCKETS

TOTAL MELTDOWN

can't sleep. And neither can Fred, who's still thinking about Angus.

'Hey, I've got something that will cheer you up.'

I climb out of bed and take a bag out of my suitcase. My Fred Alert Kit, designed to make Fred feel at home when he's away.

'It's your dinosaur pillowcase from home. And a fresh towel from the airing cupboard that Mum always wraps you in. Oh, and a picture of a Giant African Land Snail.'

'I've got something for you too. **A STAN KIT.**'

He gets out of bed, grabs his rucksack and drags it across the floor, then empties it onto the duvet.

'Oh. My. God,' I whisper, unable to believe what's in front of me.

'I brung you Mum's bestest watch so you can tell me when it's time for bed; the back door key so you can lock us up and keep us safe; the remote control for the telly so we don't miss our programmes; and the dead fly off the landing.'

'That's . . . lovely,' I whimper, knowing
Mum and Dad will be going crazy back home
trying to find all this stuff. Apart from the
dead fly. 'I'll just put those in my rucksack.'

I'm about to get back into bed when
I spot something familiar on the
windowpane.

'Fred! Look!'

He rushes out of bed, reaches up his
hand, and gently pulls at the snail stuck to
the glass.

'THIS IS THE BESTEST DAY OF MY
WHOLE LIFE!' he laughter-cries, holding
up a snail next to my eye. A snail with a
splodged felt-tip A on his shell.

Fred's face is suddenly lit from inside,
like Christmas morning.

'How did he get in here?'

I watch Fred jump for joy from one bed
to the other, as all the things in his pyjama
pockets fall out. And I realize Angus must
have fallen out when he threw the worms

COOL-O-METER

SUPERCOOL

CHILLING OUT

NO SWEAT

IN THE SHADE

COLD FEET

ON THIN ICE

LUKEWARM

HOT AND BOTHERED

SWEATING BUCKETS

TOTAL MELTDOWN

at Zac's head. He must have been in here all along.

I open the door and walk out onto the patio. It's stopped raining and the air is fresh and cold.

'Hey, Fred! They've all come to see you.' I grab his hand, leading him outside. The ground is covered with snails.

He crouches down and gently strokes them, introducing them to Angus.

'Do you fink Angus was trying to get outside?' Fred frowns, as Angus wiggles his tentacles towards another snail.

'Um, maybe. Snails love puddles don't they?'

'And I love Angus...' Fred wipes his nose on his pyjama sleeve, then gulps. 'So I'm going to be the bravest I've ever been, and let Angus live here forever, all happy and slimy and outside.'

He places Angus gently on the floor, strokes his shell, and just about manages to stutter goodbye as he watches him slime

away amongst his new snail friends.

'He'll love that, Fred.' I pull him in for a hug. 'That really is the bravest thing I've ever seen. And I've watched A LOT of Flint Danger.'

He looks up at me. Although he's not looking at me, he's looking past me, pointing.

'Hey, Stan! They've all come to see you, too.'

I lift my head, and my eyes fill with a thousand stars. The night sky is covered with them. And there running through the middle is a faint sky river.

The Milky Way.

COOL-O-METER

SUPERCOOL

CHILLING OUT

NO SWEAT

IN THE SHADE

COLD FEET

THIN ON ICE

LUKEWARM

HOT AND BOTHERED

SWEATING BUCKETS

TOTAL MELTDOWN

⤷ EVOLUTION

If scarecrows could evolve overnight, I'm
pretty sure they'd resemble the one standing
in the middle of camp, staring back at me
in his cool sunglasses. It's the best-dressed
scarecrow I've ever seen. Everyone's talking
about it as we gather outside.

'IS THAT ZAC'S LEATHER JACKET?'

'AND ONE OF HIS ELEVEN PAIRS OF
TRAINERS?'

It's styled in one of Zac's outfits,
complete with snail accessories.

'That's genius. Who did it?'

'I don't know,' Idris laughs. 'But I'd like
to shake their hand.'

'It's not over yet.' Mason points, as Zac
appears from the slumber shack.

There's something different about him,
and yet his clothes seem familiar: jeans

with more hole than jean, a Kermit the Frog T-shirt, flowery sunglasses, and trainers that don't quite match. He stops, looks at the scarecrow and nods slowly, as if acknowledging he's been had by the greatest super-dare ever.

'What's going on?' Mr Fisher asks, parting the sniggering crowd. 'Or do I really want to know why you've swapped clothes with a scarecrow, Mr Cassidy?'

'I, um . . .' He glances over at us. '. . . donated them, Sir. Thought I'd give the farmer the coolest scarecrow he's ever seen. To make up for the chaos I caused.'

'REALLY?' Mr Fisher doesn't even turn a different colour. 'Let's all go home, shall we?'

'Is it me, or has Fisher mellowed the more tired he's got?' Mason says, as we wheel our cases to the car park.

'Never mind that, what happened?'

'Maybe Zac's suitcase got taken in the middle of the night.' Tash shrugs.

'Maybe when he woke up all he had to

COOL-O-METER

SUPERCOOL
CHILLING OUT
NO SWEAT
IN THE SHADE
COLD FEET
THIN ON ICE
LUKEWARM
HOT AND BOTHERED
SWEATING BUCKETS
TOTAL MELTDOWN

wear was a box of lost property stuff.'
Maddie also shrugs.

'No way! But that would have taken a lot
of planning . . .'

As the puddles evaporate in the sun, Mr
Fisher says goodbye to Petra and Rufus,
and I mentally say goodbye to Mr Fisher's
knees, grateful I'll never see them again.
Freddie runs around saying goodbye to
everything.

'I will miss you tiny ladybird with your
bleeding knees, and poor wood meeces with
no tails.'

'You'll be back sooner than you think.'
Rufus ruffles his hair. 'And if not, you
can always bring the countryside to you.
Everything you need to know is in this
magical paper data.'

He hands him a leaflet.

'I'll miss you forever and never,' Fred
sobs.

'How about one last snail fact?' Rufus
kneels down. 'The Japanese white-eye

snail doesn't mind getting eaten by birds, cos there's a chance it'll be pooped out somewhere new! It's like getting on an aeroplane, only instead of sitting in economy, they get to hang out in some bird intestines.'

'Woah . . . snails are the bestest.'

'Sure are. And I heard what you did for Angus—you're a gastropod champion. Look after the snails, Fred, yeah?'

'I SHALL BE A SNAIL WARRIOR AND HELP ALL THE SNAILS!' Fred shouts.

'Maybe a snail whisperer.' Petra pushes her glasses up her nose. 'I spy with my inner eye . . . an otter—extrovert, fun and intelligent, with great social skills.'

She points to Flossie, who seems more than happy with that.

'And a penguin—smart, full of compassion, a friend for life.' She winks at Jess.

'I was right!' Maddie gasps. 'You ARE a penguin!'

'Um, yeah . . .' Jess frowns, then sort

SUPERCOOL

CHILLING OUT

NO SWEAT

IN THE SHADE

COLD FEET

THIN ON ICE

COOL-O-METER

LUKEWARM

HOT AND BOTHERED

SWEATING BUCKETS

TOTAL MELTDOWN

of smiles. 'I guess I am quite partial to seafood.'

'Or maybe you're an iguana.' Petra taps Liam on the shoulder. 'A docile species that enjoys basking in the sun, and can sometimes change appearance.'

Right on cue he yawns.

'And what's this?' Petra leans down towards Fred. 'Something that may seem like a pest to humans, even though he's going about his daily business, leaving a trail wherever he goes. Yet he takes time to gaze at things truly and fully. Methinks you are a snail, Fred.'

'Yes!' He jumps in the air, as Billie runs past, sobbing that she'll never see anyone ever again.

'Don't be such a silly sausage; you only live a street away,' Flossie sighs. 'We can play unicorns forever.'

It isn't just small-year-olds who aren't sure how to make friends. Zac is stood on his own as we wait to get on the coach.

He's avoiding eye contact with everyone from behind his sunglasses.

'C'mon, Stan, there's a funny smell round here.' Liam brushes past him.

'Um, hang on,' I say, tearing Zac's diagram out of my notebook and handing it to him. 'You're right. You have got a literally brilliant brain. Who knows what you could do with it next.'

I go to walk away.

'I did this for you,' he calls after me. 'I'm s'pose to say sorry to everyone.'

He hands me a scrunched piece of paper.

COOL-O-METER

SUPERCOOL

CHILLING OUT

NO SWEAT

IN THE SHADE

COLD FEET

ON THIN ICE

LUKEWARM

HOT AND BOTHERED

SWEATING BUCKETS

TOTAL MELTDOWN

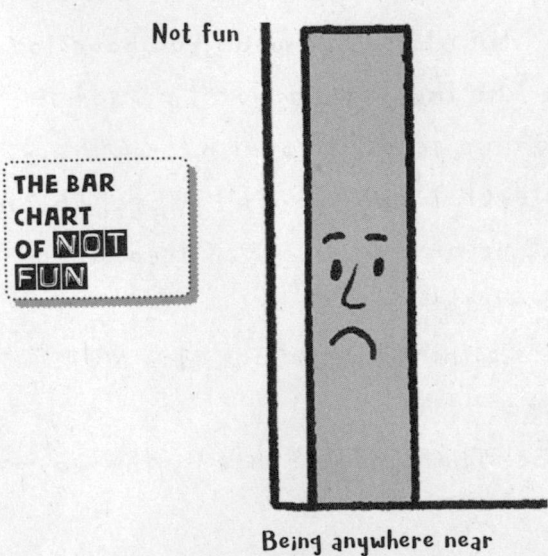

Not fun

THE BAR CHART OF NOT FUN

Being anywhere near Zac Cassidy

'Oh, um . . .'

'It's rubbish, isn't it?'

'No, but . . . if you cut out the blackmail, the boasting, the name-calling and . . . well, you could be SORT of fun.'

'I had a mate who thought I was fun once.' He shuffles his feet in the gravel. 'We did everything together—jumping over gardens, laughing at people, nicking sweets. One day he met some new mates, ones with better trainers who didn't do LAME UNITED STUFF ALL THE TIME, ZAC.'

'Are we s'pose to believe this sob story?' Idris butts in. 'Things happen to people all the time; it doesn't mean you have to behave like the world's worst person to ever go on a school trip with.'

'Whatever. I just . . . don't expect anyone to treat me nice. So I sort of treat them rubbish first.'

'Here's a thing,' Jess says. 'Try NOT doing that.'

'Maybe. That was immense by the way—

the scarecrow. Proper decent. Didn't
think you had it in you to come up with a
super-dare like that.'

'Oh that wasn't a super-dare,' Mason
says, walking over with Maddie and Tash.
He unfolds a piece of paper revealing
a complex spider diagram. 'We needed
something much more special than that . . .'

'Splans,' they all say together.

Splans are happening without my input.
It's only a matter of time before Chart Geeks
take over the world. I secretly punch the air.

'Did you wash AT ALL?' Mum cries,
attacking our faces with a mum-spit
tissue the minute we're through the door.

'I didn't!' Fred shouts proudly. 'It was the
bestest time of my life. And no way was
I Mum and Dad sick. And I didn't have to
drink my own pee.'

'Smashing,' Mum sighs, relieved at the
last statement. 'Let's unpack and I'll run

COOL-O-METER

SUPERCOOL

CHILLING OUT

NO SWEAT

IN THE SHADE

COLD FEET

ON THIN ICE

LUKEWARM

HOT AND BOTHERED

SWEATING BUCKETS

TOTAL MELTDOWN

you a bath. You both smell of campfire and
really bad socks.'

She flips open Freddie's case.

'OH. MY. GIDDY. AUNT!' She recoils in horror.

'What is it?' I leap up and look inside.

His suitcase is ALIVE.

There are slugs and snails stuck to the lid,
ladybirds and worms in his socks, beetles and
spiders crawling over his T-shirts, and woodlice
hiding in his shorts. There are sticks, flowers,
and feathers scattered in between his pants,
and dirt and leaves in every pair of shoes.

'AND I brung home a devil's coach horse,
which isn't a coach or a horse, but a beetle
that squirts stinky stuff out of its tummy.'

He's literally transported the whole
countryside home with him.

'I'm going to need A LOT of Mum
O'clock after this—at least a whole box
set of costume drama,' Mum sighs. 'You
should NEVER remove anything from the
countryside, Fred. How would you feel if an
enormous hand scooped you up and put you

down somewhere you didn't belong?'

'What, like when you dump me at Auntie Julie's?'

'That is NOT the same.'

She has to take him to the nearest park, along with all the creatures, and release them back into the wild. Unfortunately, she doesn't release Fred.

IDRIS VOICEOVER: *'HERE IN THE DEEPEST COUNTRYSIDE, WE FIND FRED DANGER—'*

'FRED THE SNAIL WHISPERER!'

'—ON ANOTHER INTREPID EXPEDITION.'

The camera pans round and zooms in on Fred, up to his elbows in worms and snails.

'I BEEN LIVING UNDER THE HEDGE AND TURNING MY GARDEN INTO A COUNTRYSIDE. HERE IS A HOLE IN THE FENCE SO HEDGEPOGS CAN GET IN. OVER THERE IS A TEENY POND FOR

COOL-O-METER

SUPERCOOL

CHILLING OUT

NO SWEAT

IN THE SHADE

COLD FEET

ON THIN ICE

LUKEWARM

HOT AND BOTHERED

SWEATING BUCKETS

TOTAL MELTDOWN

WHIRLIGIGS. THESE ARE SOME FLOWERS
FOR THE LADYBIRDS. AND RIGHT BY
DAD'S 'SCUSTING LETTUCES IS ANGUS
LAND WHERE THE SNAILS CAN LIVE.'

Petra and Rufus gave him instructions on
how to turn the garden into a wildlife haven.

'TODAY I'M PLANTING A BISCUIT
TREE,' he takes out a Jammie Dodger and
buries it. 'SOON IT WILL GROW BIG AND
STRONG LIKE MY SOCKS TREE, REMOTE
CONTROL TREE, AND CAR KEYS TREE, SO
WHEN STUFF GETS LOST WE CAN PICK
ANOTHER ONE.'

I make a mental note to dig up the
household contents before Mum notices
things have gone missing again.

I set off for Halliway Hill and an afternoon
of go-karting with no brakes. Everyone's

there, including our new mates from Larkfield. But not Zac. He moved to live with his mum by the sea. Though he did put a chart through my door before he left:

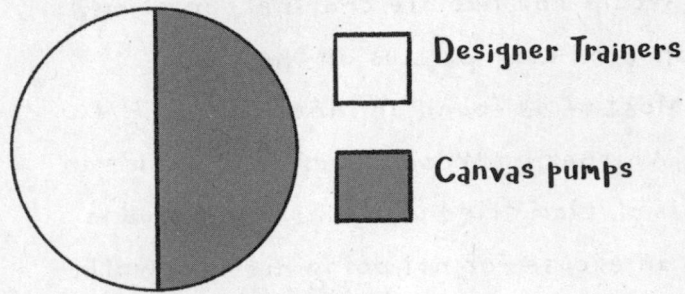

ACCEPTABLE THINGS TO WEAR ON YOUR FEET

☐ Designer Trainers

■ Canvas pumps

'Hey, Stan!' Mason shouts. 'I did another diagram!'

He hands me a piece of paper.

The Evolution of Mason Donovan

COOL-O-METER

SUPERCOOL

CHILLING OUT

NO SWEAT

IN THE SHADE

COLD FEET

ON THIN ICE

LUKEWARM

HOT AND BOTHERED

SWEATING BUCKETS

TOTAL MELTDOWN

'Blimey! You're getting a bit good at this.' I take a brand new notebook out of my rucksack. 'I think it's time you had one of these.'

'Does this make me a fully-fledged Chart Geek?'

'Woah! You two are chartners in crime, man-bro.' Liam pats us on the back.

Most of us found an inner SOMETHING at Whispering Woods, even if it wasn't an animal. Liam tried using his inner iguana as an excuse for not doing his homework, but forgot Mr Fisher's inner animal was a cranky warthog. And Fred embraced his inner snail, and promised no more ladybird beards, to the relief of everybody, but especially ladybirds and their knees.

I was happy to find my inner Stan again, and realize it's alright to be me.

'You make a better Stan than you do a Liam, that's for sure,' Jess says, climbing into the go-kart. 'And please, no more Stan words, OK?'

'Maybe one more . . . **THAT'S ONE SMALL STEP FOR STAN,**' I shout after her as she races down the hill, '**ONE GIANT LEAP FOR STANKIND!**'

COOL-O-METER

SUPERCOOL
CHILLING OUT
NO SWEAT
IN THE SHADE
COLD FEET
ON THIN ICE
LUKEWARM
HOT AND BOTHERED
SWEATING BUCKETS
TOTAL MELTDOWN

SLICES OF THANK-YOU TO

JULIA CHURCHILL for all the wonderful Bibbidi-Bobbidi-Boo that only an Agent Fairy Godmother can do.

The wonderful wizards of **OUP** for all that goes on behind the curtain. To Kathy Webb, Hannah Penny, and Fraser Hutchinson for guiding me along the yellow brick road to find my brains and courage; Holly Fulbrook and Chris Judge for bringing the heart of Stan to life.

To all of **STANKIND**—the daydreamers, the stargazers, the quiet ones at the back—one day I'll be reading your books.

GEORGE & ALEX, who I now look up to in more ways than one. Love you to Pluto and back.

PAT & KEITH —the loveliest in-laws in the land who always have a cuppa to hand, and who have been happily married for **375** years near enough.

PAUL for sharing life, box-sets, and, crucially, Maltesers with me. Couldn't have done any of this without you (and your smiley eyes) xx

MUM for just about everything (obvs), and **LAZ** for building my Plotting Shed, where I dream up stories. So yes, you practically wrote this book. Love you both heaps and heaps.

The best bits of **TWITTER**—writers, illustrators, SCBWI peeps, book-bloggers, librarians, booksellers, and teachers—your friendship and support makes the job of being a writer a lot less lonely and a lot more fabulous!

The **WATTYS!** Kas and Robert for the cheers and beers through the years; Sarah for being my (ssh) Book Organiser; and Connor for the ace spider diagram.

ABOUT THE AUTHOR

Elaine's school reports often said she was far too quiet and a bit of a daydreamer, but that's because she was too busy thinking up stories thank you very much.

Nowadays she likes to think of herself as a professional daydreamer, and spends most of her time in the Plotting Shed at the bottom of the garden where all her ideas germinate.

Elaine lives in Oxford with her telescope, husband, two sons, and loads of books.

Find out more on her website:

www.elainewickson.co.uk

ABOUT THE ILLUSTRATOR

Chris Judge is an illustrator, artist and children's picture book author from Dublin, Ireland. Chris has published several picture books since 2011 and illustrated several texts including the **DANGER IS EVERYWHERE** series with David O'Doherty and Roddy Doyle's latest children's book **BRILLIANT**. He also makes the **CREATE YOUR OWN ADVENTURE BOOKS** with his brother Andrew.

Interesting facts: Chris used to play the bass guitar in a band called **THE CHALETS** many years ago and he is allergic to carrots.